DETROIT PUBLIC LIBRARY

3 5674 05733256 2

Duffle Bag Bitches 5

By

Alicia Howard

CHANDLER PARK LIBRARY
12800 HARPER
DETROIT, MI 48213

D1529014

OCT - - 2018   CP

Duffle Bag Bitches 5

© 2015 Alicia Howard

All rights reserved. No part of this book may broadcast in

any form or without written permission from the author. With

exceptions to reviewers, magazine articles, newspaper, radio host.

Have my permission to quote pieces of my book for public display.

Chapter 1

"Slow down I don't understand what the hell you are saying." Dallas saw the strange look on Zane face as he talked on the phone. He was chilling in his office with Dizzy and Zane. They were having a few drinks before it was time to jet.

They didn't have to be there until the next morning, yet they decided that it was best to creep off in the middle of the night. The crew was waiting for Mack to show up. He said he had to handle something.

"It's Shannon, she is hurt! Shannon..." Jay was trying her best to tell him what happen to Shannon. Tasha whipped into the hospital parking lot. She took a minute to get their cause she was crying, it made it hard for her to see.

"What the fuck is wrong with my wife?" He yelled cutting Jay off. He didn't know what was going on. His heart was beating a mile a minute.

"She's bleeding; we don't know if she's going to make it." Jay didn't know that a woman could bleed that much from her woman part. The shit was freaking her out. She just knew that Shannon would bleed to death in the back seat of the truck.

Jay knew it was a possibility all could lose their life in this line of work. Yet to see a friend so close was mind boggling she was rethinking the life she lived. Her head was playing all kind of tricks. She could hear herself saying *"Do you want to die in these streets? How much money do you need before it's enough? Do you want kids and a husband?"* Jay never thought about shit like this.

Tasha was yelling at the nurse "Get her a fucking doctor now!" The nurse was trying to ask questions that no one was in the mood to answer.

"Ma'am can you tell me what happened to her?" the nurse asked.

"Bitch did you hear what the fuck she said? Get her a fucking doctor." Jay yelled.

"If my sister die out here you're going with her bitch." Jasmine said.

"Ma'am I am only doing my job the transporters are on the way down here." She was holding a clip board wondering what was caused this lady to bleed like this from her private area.

"Bitch she is pregnant help her!" Jay yelled as she held the phone to her ear.

"Ma'am I am doing all that I can. Yelling and being ignorant isn't going to help her any faster." The nurse said.

This smart mouth bitch didn't know what the fuck she was up against. She was about to get her muthafuckin ass lit up out right in front of the emergency entrance. Mack pulled up just in time. He jumped out the whip grabbing Jasmine as she was about to hit the nurse in the face. The nurse threw her hand up like she was ready to throw hands.

"No wait!" He held Jasmine by the waist to keep her from hitting the lady. "Ma'am can you please get us some help." He asked her.

"Looking I am doing the best I can. I don't have time for this ghetto shit." She looked at Jasmine "Baby girl don't let these scrubs fool

5

you. I am about that life; now can someone please tell me what is wrong with her?" The nurse flexed.

Shannon double over *"Argggggghhhhhhh."* The pain was unbelievable. She thought her whole coochie was about exit her body. She knew that she shouldn't have ignored the pains, it was too late now. Most of all she could hear this bitch talking shit instead of helping her. Shannon yelled out "Bitcchhhh I am killing you when I get out of this pain." The nurse wasn't feeling the way the crew was coming at her. She was about to speak. *Bam!* Tasha punched the bitch square in the face knocking her ass out cold.

She turned to Mack, "Pick her up; we not gone fuck let her die in this muthafucka." Mack was shocked as he let Jasmine grabbed Shannon carrying her into the hospital. She had blood everywhere it pained him to see her that way.

As Mack carried her in Tasha ran in yelling "We need of fucking doctor now!" One of her old home girls was working in the ER. She spotted Tasha then yelled.

"Aye T bring her this way." Tasha was relieved. She knew that one of the bitch she used to work with had to be there.

Jasmine and Jay entered the hospital after stomping they nurse bitch outside out a little more.

Jay forgot she was on the phone until she heard Dallas yell her name. "Jay what the fuck is going on?" Zane had dropped the phone and fell to his knees. When he heard Shannon might not make it he lost it. Zane didn't know how she could do this to him. She wasn't supposed to be working; he knew this wasn't just a mistake. He knew that Shannon was hard-headed. She was always doing shit she had no business doing. He was confused and hurt by the news.

"Dallas we're at Barnes Jewish Hospital, get here now," She hung up. Jay didn't want to keep trying to explain what the hell was going on over the phone. "We on the way." Dallas assured her yet she didn't hear him. Tasha was talking to her home girl Candy, who informed her that Shannon was rushed to surgery. She told her she wasn't sure if the baby would make it. As Tasha thanked her for helping them an officer approached her.

Mack peeped it and he gave Jay and Jasmine the key to get the fuck out of there. He knew they didn't want to, but they had no choice after stomping the girl out.

He walked over to Tasha as the officer tapped her. He saw Jay and Jasmine hauling ass. "Ma'am can I ask your name?" the officers asked.

"No you may not if I am not under arrest." Tasha told him.

Her friend walked away. Tasha was her girl, but she wasn't trying to lose her job. Candy had four kids to feed now that she was out the stripper game. This was her only bread and butter. She planned to keep her eye on Shannon, and this sexy nigga standing beside Tasha.

"Ma'am you under arrest for the assault of Patricia Brown." He grabbed her to handcuff her.

Tasha laughed as he handcuffed her. She couldn't believe after all the shit she had done wrong in her life. She would get locked the first time trying to save a muthafuckas life. All she could do was laugh.

"Ma'am this is not a laughing matter." The officer said.

"It is to me." Tasha told him, Candy was watching. She'd never seen Tasha so bold. The girl was rather shy at time, kind a push over. She wondered what brought about the change in her.

The officer got a little angry, "We will see if you're still laughing once you're behind bars." He grabbed her up.

"Man what the fuck you on?" Mack asked he was pissed. He knew they were going to try to pull bullshit like this.

"Sir you need to stand back." The officer looked him up and down.

He laughed thinking he had to play it cool because he didn't want to leave Shannon here alone. Tasha looked at him, "Baby it's cool." She assured him.

He kissed her. "Baby you will be out soon as they set the bond," He assured her.

Chapter 2

Dallas, Zane, and Dizzy rushed in just as Tasha was being handcuffed. They spotted them and Zane rushed over to Mack. "Bruh tell me my baby good!" He said with tears in his eyes.

"Bruh she's in surgery." Mack told him grabbing his man and hugging him because he didn't want to see him cry. Dallas brought their attention back to Tasha.

"What's going on here?" He asked watching the officer handcuff Tasha.

"She's under arrest for assaulting a nurse." The office said.

"I don't think you want to book her if you plan to have a job in the morning." Dallas assured him as he dialed a number on his phone.

"You don't have the pull to get me fired," The officer said. He didn't know who this guy thought he was, but that street cred crap didn't mean shit to him.

Mack winked at Tasha as her home girl Candy watched what was taking place and she smiled. Her pussy was wet from all the power and tension in the room. Dallas dialed a number and spoke in codes, then hung up to wait for results.

The officer's radio went off, "Officer Baxter."

"Yes Captain," He answered looking at Dallas strangely.

"Let the young lady go; we will compensate the nurse another way. It's an emotional time for that family, and it was a misunderstanding. She never meant to harm anyone. She was just trying to save her sister's life," He said.

"Are you serious?" Baxter couldn't believe this shit. He was angry this bitch was getting off the hook. She smiled with a smug ass look and he wanted to knock her ass out.

"As a heart attack," The Captain told him. He wasn't fucking around with Baxter's bullshit today. He was making too much money with Dallas.

"But…." Baxter said.

"But my ass! Un-cuff her now….do you read me? I am not fucking around I'll have your badge if you don't let her go." the captain assured.

"10-4." Baxter let her go. He pushed her as he released her.

"Bitch ass nigga!" Tasha yelled. Tasha's friend couldn't believe the shit her eyes had just seen. She didn't know what type of nigga Tasha had gotten down with but all she knew was that she wanted in. She was planning to do everything she could to make sure that happen.

She watched as the man un-cuffed Tasha and realized the bitch was sporting top shelf designer clothing, jewelry, and shoes. She knew the bitch had stopped working at the strip club and the hospital. So she knew this fine ass nigga standing by her was holding big figures.

Tasha walked over to Dallas kissing him on the cheek then she went to help Mack console Zane. Candy watched Dallas and she could tell he was the top dog. He would never check for a girl like her. Yet Mack on the other side was the nigga that liked bottom feed type bitches. She was plotting to use everything in her power to take this nigga from Tasha. Money is more valuable than friendship.

Shannon had been in surgery for what seemed like forever. When the doctor came out calling for the Dunn family Jasmine jumped up first catching the doctor's attention. "Hey over here," She waved.

Jay had called Mack to see was the coast clear. Once he informed her what went down with cops, they doubled back. Jasmine had to be there with her sister no matter what. She would go to jail if she had to. She just wants to know that her sister was okay.

The doctor walked over to the bunch. A few still covered in blood, all wearing top of the line designer. He didn't know for sure what they did for a living. Yet if he had to guess it was illegal. It often shocked him women were caught up in the lifestyle; often more so than men.

He looked at Jasmine's beautiful face thinking of all the things she could be. Model, singer, dance, or actor. Hell she could even be a doctor or lawyer. Yet here she was amongst thugs/gangstas. "Who are you to her?" He asked before giving her any information out.

He knew that crews that ran together like this consider themselves family. But if no one was a blood relative here there would be nothing he could tell them until they bring someone in who was.

"I am her sister." Jasmine reached for Zane grabbing him by the hand pulling him up front with her. "This is Zane, her soon to be husband, father of the baby." She told the doctor.

Dallas was trying to stay focused. He wanted to hear what the doctor had to say but Venom was blowing his phone up like she was crazy. He didn't have the time to see what she wanted. He was dealing with life and death at the moment.

"Sir do you want me to speak to you in private or can I speak freely here?" Doctor Rodriguez asked.

"We're family here, just lay the shit on the table Doc." Zane walked away not facing him. He was still close enough to hear what was being said. Mack walked over by him hoping that everything was cool.

"Shannon is stabilized now, it's been touch and go. We're not sure if she is going to make it. While we were getting the baby out she slipped into a coma. I don't know when or if she will come out of it at all. For the time being we have her on meds and life support.

At this moment we are just trying to keep her comfortable. The baby is also stabilized for the moment as well.

She only weights three pounds, we have her on tube feeding and life support as well. It is not going to be an easy task, only time will tell what the outcome of your family will be Zane." He hated to share this news, yet it was a part of his job.

By the time he was done all the women were crying, and the men looked confused. "I don't think it's best all of you stay here tonight. Visiting hours are over since Jasmine is a blood relative she gets to decide if she or Zane will stay with Shannon overnight," He said.

"I love my sister," Jasmine cried. "I know that Zane need to be here with his family. I will come back in the morning." She cried falling in to Dizzy's arms.

He didn't know how to handle the hurt he was feeling. It saddens him that Shannon was fighting for her life. Yet the pain on Jasmine bothered him even more. He loves this woman more than he loved himself.

Zane walked over to Jasmine, "Sis we're going to get past this, we've been through some tough shit." He pointed to Mack. "You see that man there? He is walking proof that we can beat this."

Tasha cried as she held on to Mack thinking about how she almost lost him. Jasmine looked at him as well knowing Zane was right. His love would keep Shannon alive. Tasha's love kept Mack alive she believed. All that really mattered was that he was here with her.

"You're right bruh." Jasmine hugged him then ran out the hospital. Tasha and Jay followed her. They had to make sure their girl was good. It was hard to go through this without her husband or children by her side.

Jay was glad that Dizzy was there for Jasmine, but something in the pit of her stomach told her it would not be enough.

Chapter 3

Dizzy watched her run out, he wanted to follow her yet he let the girls do it. He needed to make sure that Zane was okay. Dallas, Zane, and Mack all stood there lost for words. They stayed that way until they heard the doctor say "Are you ready for me to take you back?"

Zane looked at him, "No, but I have no choice." A tear finally slipped from his eye. His three home boys all hugged him at once. He needed their strength to help him do this. As the group hugged, Mack prayed.

"God I know you don't fuck with me like that, but I am back again asking for your mercy and grace. Forgive me for cursing when I pray I am just a sinner that heard you love us all. It's my sister. I know why you want her, because she's the angel that up and ran away from heaven. We need her, most of all Zane needs you. Father hear us when we pray. Amen."

"Amen." The other men chimed.

The doctor watched he was amazed at the level of love he had seen so many thugs share with each other. He knew that hood love was special whether it was between a man and his woman or homies; it's a ride or die love that most family members never share with each other.

As the men let go the doctor waited for Zane. He walked over to the doctor, "I am ready." He wasn't, but he had to be.

"Aye man if you need me just call and I am here." Dallas knew the business trip must be postponed.

"Me too man," Dizzy said. He knew what it was like to lose a wife and child. He didn't have his own family at the moment and that bothered him. He needed to change his life.

Zane nodded trying to keep from crying. He was blessed to have niggas in his life that really had his back. He didn't know where he would be without these guys. He never really had time to tell them how much he loved and appreciated them.

Once he got things in order with his wife he plans to tell them. His tears betrayed him in front of his boys as they fell against his will.

"Man take your little cry baby ass back there. Be strong for my sister and niece nigga," Mack said. He made jokes out of everything in life because it was the only way he knew how to deal with his emotions.

Zane laughed, "Fuck you bitch nigga." As he walked off with the doctor he heard Mack yell,

"Bitch nigga I love you too!" Mack ran out the hospital. He needed Tasha to hold him. Zane smiled as he took the journey to see his wife and child fight for their life.

The sunshine through Dizzy's bedroom window fell upon Jasmine's face. She could smell breakfast cooking. She smiled on the inside, but the expression on the outside of her face didn't match. She had spoken to her mother Marilyn after she left Shannon at the hospital. Her mother didn't trip off the hustle they were on; she had done her own dirt in the past. She didn't judge her children. She'd taught them right from wrong, but this was their life to live.

Jasmine could hear her mother ask her, *"Are you sure that you gone let your husband go forever?"* She had never thought about forever. One thing about her mother, she knew how to get into your head and business without you knowing.

Jasmine's sister Alicia hated when their mom did that, but that was moms. Now she had to deal with the question at hand. Her husband wasn't no saint; hell neither was she.

She hopped out the bed grabbing her clothing and got dressed. She need to talk to her husband; like right now. She didn't know what he wanted to do, but it was time to figure all this shit out. She could no longer use money as an excuse for doing the shit she was doing.

The truth was she was doing it because she loved the excitement you often missed out on when you get married and have children too early in life. It's best to find out who the fuck you are and wanted to be before dedicating your life to one another.

She loved her children with all her heart. As she thought about that, her niece Jailah entered her mind. She had to deal with her mother fight for her life. Most five year olds wouldn't understand what that meant, but Jailah did. The devil had been trying to take that baby out since the day she came into this world. Shannon had a horrible birth with Jailah. The child was fine, but we didn't know if Shannon would make it.

Then when Jailah was three she slipped off the third floor balcony of Jasmine's old apartment building. Jasmine just knew that she was dead, but God caught her in mid-air placing her on the second floor balcony. She walked away with the wind knocked out of her for a minute, and a huge knot on her head.

Tears fell from Jasmine's eyes as she remembered this. Now to know that Shannon was fighting for her life again how could she be so selfish? Why would she do this to her kids? Husband?

Dizzy entered the room to wake her, yet he found her stuffing her feet into her shoes.

"Where are you going?" He asked.

She looked up at him with tear stained face. "Home," She said.

She knew the words cut him like a knife. Jasmine didn't want to hurt him; she knew that he had been hurt enough already. She had let this thing between them go too far.

"Home huh?" He said as his heart beat hard in his chest. He sat down on the bed he felt like he would have a heart attack. He had a feeling this day would come. He was just hoping that it never did. Yet here it was, it was nothing he could do to stop it.

"Yes home!" She yelled, but not because she was mad at him. It was because she was mad at herself. For all the bullshit she caused for no reason. She had hurt her husband, children, and now Dizzy. She wondered what kind of monster she was. *How could I be so heartless?* She questioned herself.

"Why are you yelling? I should be the muthafucka mad." Dizzy jumped off the bed punched wall. He couldn't believe he allowed this shit to happen to him. Jasmine stood frozen in her tracks crying.

"I am sorry! I never meant for things to end this way. I never meant to hurt you, I love you. It's just I made a huge mistake." she cried.

"Just go home Jasmine. I hope you doing this for you and not because of what Shannon is going through. I don't think you know what you want, but it's up to you to find it." He walked into the bathroom to attend to the bloody knuckles he had from hitting the wall.

Jasmine stood there crying because she didn't know why she was doing this. She just knew that it was time to deal with all the issues of her life. The thought of losing Shannon opened her eyes to what was going on in her own world. She should fix it, so she just prayed as she walked out the bedroom to leave hoping Dizzy would forgive her someday.

As Dizzy heard the door slam he closed his eyes. He could feel his heart break like shattered glass. He wanted to blame Jasmine, but his truth wouldn't allow him to do that. He had no rights to her. He knew that she was married. He had played the game, too bad he lost.

Chapter 4

John Legend's song "All of Me" spilled from the speakers in Mack's bedroom on this early morning.

What would I do without your smart mouth

Drawing me in, and you kicking me out

You got my head spinning, no kidding, I can't pin you down

What's going on in that beautiful mind

I'm on your magical mystery ride

And I'm so dizzy, don't know what hit me, but I'll be alright

My head's underwater

But I'm breathing fine

You're crazy and I'm out of my mind

Mack kissed Tasha's body so softly and gentle as she laid on her back. He could tell by the way her eyes rolled in the back of her head she was loving this love making shit. He had to admit that he liked it too a little bit. He loved the way his soft touches made her body shiver and tears to flow from her eyes.

He thought that shit only happened in movies. "Hmmmm," Tasha moaned as Mack licked the inside of her thighs and teased her throbbing pussy by blowing hot air on it.

"Girl cut that moaning shit out girl I ain't even kissed her yet," He smiled. That sexy smile at her caused her pussy to cream even more. Mack couldn't believe that he was eating pussy because he vowed to never do no shit like that in his life. Tasha was the only woman to experience this. The music continued to play.

'Cause all of me

Loves all of you

Love your curves and all your edges

All your perfect imperfections

Give your all to me

I'll give my all to you

You're my end and my beginning

Even when I lose I'm winning

Cause I give you all of me

And you give me all of you, oh

How many times do I have to tell you

Even when you're crying you're beautiful too

The world is beating you down, I'm around through every

mood

You're my downfall, you're my muse

My worst distraction, my rhythm and blues

I can't stop singing, it's ringing in my head for you

My head's underwater

But I'm breathing fine

You're crazy and I'm out of my mind

As John Legend continued to serenade them Mack parted Tasha pussy lips with his tongue. She was wet, sticky, and sweet. He slurped her pussy like it was the last supper. She wiggled, moaned, and tried to run, but he locked her ass in place. She had him hooked on sucking her pussy now. "Mack, oh Mack, oh shit baby! Youuuu youuuuuu ohhhhh shit," Tasha moaned.

Mack lifted his head. "Girl cut all that shit out. You know this my jam and I am trying to eat," Mack winked at her. She giggled. She loved this so much. He was so crazy, but she loved every moment. Mack continued to please her this morning as the song played.

'Cause all of me

Loves all of you

Love your curves and all your edges

All your perfect imperfections

Give your all to me

I'll give my all to you

You're my end and my beginning

Even when I lose I'm winning

Cause I give you all of me

And you give me all of you, oh

Give me all of you, oh oh

Cards on the table, we're both showing hearts

Risking it all though it's hard

Cause all of me

Loves all of you

Love your curves and all your edges

All your perfect imperfections

Give your all to me

I'll give my all to you

You're my end and my beginning

Even when I lose I'm winning

Cause I give you all of me

And you give me all of you

I give you all of me

And you give me all, of you, oh oh oh.

By the end of the song Tasha had Mack's head locked in place with her legs as she came all down his throat. "OMGGGGGGGGGGGG," Tasha screamed as legs went limp.

"Damn right call on the lord." Mack got out the bed to go brush his teeth. Tasha was still on the bed shivering. Mack had been eating that pussy all night and morning. He wouldn't give her the dick no matter how much she begged last night. He felt funny beating her walls down after seeing Shannon bleeding like that.

Tasha was finally about to speak, "Baby you a beast with that mouth, but I still want dick." She was a horny bandit so this baby had to be a boy. She thought no girl would make her this horny.

"Girl your ass just stop shaking; I am not fucking with you. I am about to go check on my brother. I know he dealing with some shit seeing his wife in the hospital," Mack told her.

"I am sorry we didn't tell y'all about that dude Nick B. I just wanted to make the girls trust me. I want them to look at me as family." Her body was feeling great from the loving her man had put on her, yet she wanted him to know that she knew she violated not telling him.

"You were wrong for that, but I will give you a pass this time because you were gaining your stripes. Next time I will have to tap that ass." He came out the bathroom jumping into black jogging pants, tank top, and Subzero Jordan's. He was causally sexy for his hospital visit.

"I will come with you." Tasha said.

"No you are supposed to be lying low!" Mack told her.

"Why? Cause I didn't tell you what was going down?" She flopped back down on the bed.

"First of all watch how you handle my baby. Second kill the fucking attitude. Lastly you were the person to lure dude into that building. If it's only the front entrance camera they still have something on you. I am sure the girls covered your ass. Until we know for sure, this is where the fuck you will be, whether you're like it or not. Do you understand?" Mack couldn't believe she had the nervous to question to him.

"Yes," She pouted.

"You still got the damn attitude," He said.

"I am sorry baby," She said.

"Whatever," He was pissed now and talked shit as he walked out the door. *"What happened to women want to cook and take care of home? Now women want to be Zena the princess warrior and Charlie's Angel's and shit. Need to get their ass somewhere and sit the fuck down,"* Tasha heard as the door slammed.

Tasha got up to clean the house and prepared a home cooked meal for her man. Hoping would place him back in her good graces. She knew his fussing was from being scared of what happened to Shannon would or could happen to her. He never planned for her to be a part of the team. Yet she wanted to prove herself.

Now that she was in good with the girls. She was good, now she better gets her home front back where it needs to be.

Chapter 5

Dallas was holding for Venom which he didn't like. He was a boss; he didn't hold for no damn one yet Venom was his bawss. You couldn't call her office and hang up unless she told the receptionist she would call you back. If that wasn't the case, you held on until you were told to otherwise.

He was looking at his watch and thinking about Kim. He didn't know what this new found fondness with love was, but he was enjoying for now. He was going to have to give her sexy ass a call sometimes today.

"Why I am talking to you on the phone instead of in person?" Venom was pissed. She had just came from a meeting with Vicious asking her what happened to her team. She didn't like for her sister to question her, or feel as if her team must handle this. Yes, they were retired, but came out in emergencies.

"One of my girls are down, well she was already down for pregnancy…" Venom cut Dallas off.

"If she was down why the fuck aren't you here?" she was confused.

"It's not that simple. She went out on a local mission and got hurt. Her husband couldn't leave her here alone." Dallas knew that Venom didn't take no shorts for business.

"Was this mission your orders?" she asked because she wasn't aware of any local hit.

He didn't want to answer this question. Dallas knew that Venom is a by the book type of bitch. She taught him that when you follow rules it kept you out of jail and hell. "No."

"A hard head makes a soft ass my nigga." She said with a chuckle.

He thought back on when he asked her how to handle Nisha's hard headed ass. She told him to have her beat up, but not killed then make her think he put rules in place for her safety.

"I know. She's closer to me then the last one was. Her husband is my right hand V, cut a nigga a muthafuckin break. I ain't never fucked up on business or asked for no favors." Dallas was pissed now. He hated her overbearing shit sometimes.

"Aye watch how you talk to a lady," She said.

"Act like a fucking lady then, have some damn compassion," He said not thinking about her feelings.

34

"I wasn't born with a dick, but life made me stronger than most men. Forgive a bitch for not being sentimental. I see this important to you. I will give you two weeks to clean this shit up. That's all I can give, do you respect that?" Venom asked.

She was a little hurt by the words of her lack of compassion, but she would never tell him that.

"Thank you and I apologize. I should have never said that to you. I know you were dealt a raw hand in life," He told her.

"Thanks Dee," She said.

"Anytime baby. I am going to make it count for you," He assured her.

"I know you will," Venom said to him.

She had been down with Dallas for many years never had he crossed her. Even though she chewed him out she knew it was something important for him to flack on her.

"In a minute baby," He said to her.

"Not a second later," She laughed at the old terms they used.

Dallas got off the phone with her then called Kim. He needed love in the worst way right about now. Venom had giving him two weeks to get shit in order. He was going to spend a few days with Kim.

"Hello," Kim said.

"Hey baby," Dallas said in a sad voice.

"What the matter?" she asked.

"Nothing," He said. He didn't know how to share his feeling with a woman.

"It don't sound like nothing." She wanted to pick him apart. She knew the nigga like a book so she wasn't buying it.

"I need you baby," He said.

"I am on the next red eye." Kim didn't need him to ask her twice.

"Thank you," Dallas said.

"I love you." She wanted him to know that she was there for him.

"I love you to baby, see you when you get here," Dallas hung up with smile on his face.

He knew he needed to rest before Kim comes but he had to call and check up on Zane. He didn't want his man's thinking he was going through this shit alone.

Jasmine pulled into the drive way of Korey's house. She was still crying from leaving Dizzy's house. She'd fell in love with him. She knew that she was wrong for allowing things to get this far. Now her sister was in the hospital fighting for her life. She felt like she was letting her life fall apart behind the thrill, excitement, and money.

"Fuck you!" she yelled at herself. She didn't know how she was going to make this shit right. Dallas had given her a pass a long time ago. If she had taken the pass leaving the game behind things would've never gotten this far. She was so deep in thought she didn't see Korey pull up.

"How did I let this shit get this far?" she asked herself. Jasmine cried her eyes out for all the wrong she had done. She wished she could turn back the hands of the time. Dizzy didn't deserve this nor did her husband. She was way out of line for the shit she caused. Now it time to woman up and straighten this shit out.

"How far did it go?" Jasmine heard the voice asked.

Jasmine looked up not sure if she should answer that question. "Too far!" she said.

"Want to talk about it?" Korey asked. He missed his wife so much. He hoped she was ready to come home. The kids missed her and asked about her daily. Yet he missed her more; he was tired of sleeping alone. He was ready to fix it or leave it alone so he could move on.

"I think we should." She said to him with tear stained face. She wasn't ready to tell it all, yet she knew it was time to bear her soul. It was up to her husband to decide if he would still have her or not.

Korey opened the car door to help his wife out the car. He knew she was broken, and need him more than ever right now. He would be less than a husband to turn her away. No one was perfect. He had done wrong and so had she. It was time to see if the love they shared was strong enough to get past the bullshit. "Come on baby let's talk," He said.

Jasmine jumped out the car fell into his arms crying her eyes out. She felt safe at the moment, like everything wrong in the world would be all right if he was holding her. Jasmine never knew how much she missed her husband until this moment.

"It's ok love we will get through this, all you have to do is tell me when you ready," Korey assured her they can get past this.

"I am ready, I am so ready, and I am really ready." She knew it was time to change her life for her husband and children.

Chapter 6

Mack was sitting in the cafeteria eating food as Zane stared off in space. He wanted Shannon to wake up; he needed for her to come around. He needed her in his life. Life had no meaning without her. She was his rib and he couldn't go on without her. He promised her he would marry her. Why was god trying to take that away from him? He had a beautiful baby girl. Now all he needed was his wife back.

Zane cried without even knowing the tears were falling as he thought about all the good times him, and Shannon shared. The first moment he saw her he knew that she was the one. No matter how much he tried to deny it, she was the one. Everything about her made him want to be a better man.

"Nigga you can't cry like that in public," Mack told Zane handing him a tissue. Zane took it now caring who saw his hurt.

"Bruh what I am gone do if she doesn't live?" He asked Mack with desperate look in his eye.

Mack looked away for a moment because he didn't want the emotions to jump on him. "She's not going to leave you here alone man. She knows you need her, let her body get the rest it needs," Mack told him. He didn't have the heart to think about her not making it.

"I am just saying bruh what if she doesn't wake up? What I am going to do then?" Zane asked.

Mack took a deep breath, "You will take care of them girls, show them how a nigga is supposed to love them even after death." Mack had to answer the question because Zane want the real from him.

"I know, but I don't think I am strong enough to do it without her man. Why life got to be so damn hard?" He needed to know. With all the money in the world, he couldn't buy his woman's health back. He had to just wait it out to see what cards God would deal him.

Mack's phone rung before he could speak; it was Dallas. "Hello?"

"Nigga what the fuck is good with you?" Dallas asked sounding cool.

"Nigga stop calling here acting like you cool. We all fucked up out here nigga, what the hell you calling me for anyway?" He was hoping he wasn't telling him it was time to ride out. He need more time with his woman.

"Bitch I was calling to check on Zane, I knew your bitch ass would be up there." Dallas hated when Mack called him out when he was trying to play it cool.

"He over here hollering and shit," Mack said causing Zane to laugh. He loved that Mack could be an asshole even when real life was going on. He was just raw like that.

"Nigga put him on the damn phone!" Dallas wasn't in the mood for this crazy ass nigga.

"Bitch you called my shit show me some muthafuckin respect," Mack fucked with the nigga's head by talking shit.

"Fuck you," Dallas said. Mack busted out laughing then handed Zane the phone.

Zane got on the phone as he laughed inside at the bickering his two homies were doing. It was great to have people who care about your well-being in your life. He didn't want to live life without Shannon yet he knew if he had to he would be just fine. "What's up man?" He tried to hide the hurt.

"I just wanted to see how you were holding your head up." Dallas love his guys; they had been through some tough shit together. When it first started out it was just about the money. Now it was about family.

"Man you know me, I am good man," He lied. Zane didn't know what else to say. Men didn't have the relationship women have with their friends. It was hard to express the level of hurt he was dealing with to another man or anyone else.

"I thought I knew you until the day that Shannon walked into my office. I knew at the moment you laid eyes on her you'd changed into someone I didn't know. I thought the change would be for the worst, yet I must say it was the best move you've ever made in your life." Dallas felt like his ponta needed to hear that right now.

"Thanks man that means so much to me." Zane never knew love before Shannon. Loving her wasn't easy, but he wasn't no walk in the park either.

"Man I just wanted you to know if you need me I am here," Dallas said.

"That's what's up man, on another note how we looking on the business side? I know Venom is hot with us," Zane said.

"I know Ms. Mean Bitch better not have a hit out on us," Mack yelled loud enough for Dallas to hear.

Dallas laughed at his crazy ass. "Tell him she only has the hit out on him. Nah on the real she gave us two weeks to get shit in order," Dallas told him.

"I don't know if that will work for me, you know these things move on their own accord," Zane told him.

"Don't even sweat it. If you're not comfortable leaving your family I respect that. I will take the others to get this money and don't worry about missing out on the money because I will handle that for you," Dallas said.

"Good looking out man. I love you," Zane said.

"I love you too bro," Dallas said. Before he could hang up he heard Mack yell, "I love y'all more!" Dallas laughed as they hung up.

Chapter 7

Jay sat in front of the television watching the news. Shit was all bad; they had her old building on lock down. She was wondering if they had any leads on this shit involving Nick B. She was hoping the press didn't cover this shit too much. Jay knew the main reason this shit was on the news anyway was because the shit happened in an upscale neighborhood.

She was glad she didn't rent the apartment in her name. Jay used a crack head's name that had great credit. She wasn't worried about anything tracing back to her cause the bitch that rented it for her didn't even know her real name.

The real hype at the scene was all the video recording of coming and going for that day was missing. Jay called the security guard asking him to make his round early. He could do that if he thought there was funny business going on in the building. The time he was gone, gave her time to steal the tapes she need.

Mariah was sitting the chair wondering if this lady was this damn crazy for real. This woman came back to the hotel room covered in blood. She showered and went to bed. Then she woke up and canceled housekeeping service, then ordered room service. Now here she was talking to the television as she ate like Mariah wasn't in the room with her. Mariah was hungry but glad she hadn't eaten because she didn't want to shit on herself. She was already sitting in her own piss and funk. She prayed that Jay let her bath soon. Mariah thought she was a dirty bitch for how she played her uncle, but now she knew this bitch was a cold piece of work.

"Hey!" Mariah called out for her.

"Hey is for horses I know your mother taught you better than that," Jay said chewing on her bacon.

"I know you had something to do with what's going on, on the news." She said.

"So what who you gone tell if I did?" Jay munched on her toast.

"I will tell the cops," She said.

"Girl the only reason you breathing is because I am allowing you to," Jay reminded her.

Mariah hadn't realized that when she talked. It was the smell of the food clouding her brain. "I was just joking girl if you let me go I won't ever mention you," She said.

"You can't mention me anyway. You don't know who the hell I am, but you will find out." She was wondering why this stinking bitch was even bothering her at breakfast.

"I am sorry I never should have come here." She thought about that after her son died. The plan she placed in her head to shake Jay down for money was a bad idea. She could tell this was the woman you would have to kill to get her money. Now her she had been tied two a chair for the past two fucking days. Mariah knew her life couldn't be anymore fucked up.

"No you shouldn't have come here. You should have stayed out my fucking business. What I did to Cash wasn't personal Mariah, it was business. I will tell you why I deal in this business. Cause niggas don't give a fuck enough for me. You know I am not lying; you were pregnant the last time I seen you. Where's the father?" Jay was schooling her about life.

"My baby dead but the father was never around," She lowered herself thinking about how she played herself dealing with the nothing ass niggas.

Jay got pissed off thinking about how the girl's child had died. "I am sorry about the kid, but I don't feel sorry for you. You

47

the type of bitch out here look for love. I am the type bitch that love herself enough to recognize bullshit when I see it coming. So I say fuck love I am focused on the money.

I am not saying Cash was a bad dude, but he played games with a lot of bitches before he met me. I was just the one to come trump his ass. I know that don't sit well with you, but instead of being bitter I suggest you take a few rules from my book," Jay told her as she got up to pour herself a glass of orange juice.

"That was my family; you didn't have to kill him," Mariah was crying now.

"I didn't kill him, and no one else would have if he just took the loss. He couldn't live with that, so it cost him his life. I can't apologize for that cause his death wasn't my fault. I didn't want his life, I just wanted his money," Jay kept it real with her.

"You don't think about the lives attached to the people you wrong," Mariah was speaking about herself; how her life changed once he died.

"That's not a part of my job," Jay said as she got her clothing for the day ready. She would check on her girl soon. She understood how Mariah felt, yet it was all a part of the game she was in.

"So you just kill and steal with no remorse?" Mariah asked. She didn't understand cold hearted people like this. They walked around as if the owned the world.

"Tell me what remorse has gotten you little girl? You out here alone, looking assed out, uncle dead, child dead, fucking with niggas who couldn't care less. Tell me what the fuck has remorse done for you?" She was pissed at the way the world made women so weak.

"Nothing, got damn." Mariah tried to jump causing the chair to fall over. She laid on her side kicking trying to break free. She was mad because Jay was right about everything she was saying. She had been walking around remorseful and feeling sorry for herself, and she had nothing to show for it.

"That's right get mad take control of your life Mariah, I am going to take a bath." Jay stepped over the chair heading to the shower.

As Jay stood in the shower she cried for Shannon, Jasmine, Tasha, Herself, and even Mariah. It was hard being a woman this day and age. It's even harder when you try to show a nigga you're a ride or die, and he keeps testing your gangsta to see if you're capable of being broken.

We have to walk around with so many titles like mom, sister, therapist, doctor, lawyer, teacher, and friend. Yet the only time a nigga can see you be when you act like a bitch. Jay refused to let others control her life or way of thinking. If bitch was the only title of value, she planned to become the queen of bitches. She hopped out the shower ready for the world.

Jay was wondering what the hell she was going to do with Mariah. Her new place was ready, and she was about to shake this hotel. She didn't want to kill the little bitch; it wasn't her fault she knew no better. She thought about letting her run with the crew, but then she imagined a few years from now the bitch blowing her brains out.

She didn't have time to harp on it. As she left the room Mariah was still on her side. She had cried herself to sleep and all Jay could think was *"Poor baby."* Jay exited them room off to see Shannon hoping things were getting better.

Chapter 8

Tequila spotted Dizzy as he came out of his apartment. She hadn't seen him since little Ms. Pretty bitch's car was on fire. He didn't even bother to come in to pay his rent anymore; he did everything online. She could tell by his movements that something wasn't right with him.

As he was getting into his car she spoke, "Hey Dizzy." She knew she didn't know him that well but she'd heard Ms. Pretty bitch call him that.

He jumped as if he didn't walk past her getting to his car. "Hey baby I didn't see you standing there. I got a lot of shit on my mind how are you?" he asked.

"I am great; haven't seen you around in a while." She was so excited he was speaking to her in a nice tone. Tequila wished the conversation could last forever.

"Like I said baby I been dealing with so much. I am about to jet so I will check up with you later. We should hang out some time soon," He said getting into his car.

She knew this nigga wasn't in the right state of mind inviting her to hang out. She wasn't sure about what was going on with him. She planned to take him up on his offer before he snapped out of whatever trance he was in.

Dizzy speed off. His head was fucked up off what Jasmine had done today. He wanted to blame her, he needed to blame her, yet he knew that he couldn't; He was heartbroken. *"How the fuck did I let this shit happen?"* He asked. We never questioned ourselves when we do the wrong things yet they feel good. The moment the shit turns for the worst we want to question everything. Question nor answer could help the pain he felt right now.

The only thing capable of making this pain go away is the woman torn between two lives. Dizzy was afraid that she had finally chosen up it, and he could do nothing about it. He pulled into a local bar the crew would kick it at from time to time. He just wants to smoke a Cuban and have a drink. Dizzy could have gone to the club house, yet he wanted to be alone without explaining what he was dealing at the moment.

As Jay walked down the hallway to Shannon's room, she could hear the beeping from the machine. Her stomach turned as she got closer to the door. She dreads the day she had to come see her friend hooked to machines fighting for her life. Jay slowly opened the door the room was empty and freezing cold. She didn't understand what the fuck was going on.

No one had called her to tell her that Shannon didn't make it. She knew they wouldn't leave her out in the cold like that. Something was wrong. Jay came running out the room screaming, "Where is she?" "Where is she?" She was freaking out.

Mack and Zane were coming back from seeing the baby girl when they spotted Jay down on the floor screaming, "Somebody help me! Where is she?" Mack ran to Jay's side. Zane ran in to the room. It was freezing and empty. Suddenly the room spun; He was about to pass out. He fell up against the walling thinking to himself, *"This can't be happening."* He knew to find out what the hell was going on he was going to have to pull himself together.

Zane pulled himself to his feet, walking out of the room with fire in his eyes. He spotted Shannon's doctor. He walked up to the desk snatching that nigga from behind the counter lifting him off his feet.

"Where the fuck is my wife?" He looked at the doctor with death in his eyes. Mack wasn't in the mood to catch case, but when the guard came toward Zane he had to stop them. This man was trying to get information on his wife.

"Sir, sir!" the doctor yelled. He was sacred for his life.

"Tell where she is or I will snap your fucking neck." Zane knew she wasn't dead; he could feel her spirit.

"She had to be rushed back to surgery." Zane dropped him. He was hoping she would pull through; he didn't know what caused her to end up back in surgery.

The doctor knew Zane was going through a lot. He waved the guards off who was fighting with Mack. The doctor understood the pain the family was suffering with. "What caused this doc?" Mack asked.

The doctor lowered his head "Her lungs were filling up with blood. We had to get in there before she died. Right now she is stable, we can't bring her back to this room until we are sure she doesn't need more surgery. We are doing everything in our power to keep her alive," The doctor said.

"What do we have to do? What do we have to pay?" Zane asked. He was willing to lay down for her.

"The best thing you and your family can do for her is pray," The doctor said.

Jay cried as Mack held her. She couldn't believe all of this was going on. She prayed that Shannon would come around. She informed Mack she would call Jasmine to let her know what was going on. She asked him to hang around because she needed his help with something. He assured her he would be there for whatever she needed.

As Jay walked away all she heard was "Damn," followed a loud bang; Zane had punched the wall. Jay hurried down the hall to call Jasmine.

The ringing was causing Jasmine to go crazy. She was in a passionate love making session with her husband. It had been months since he had touched her body. She had forgotten why she married this man. He was playing her body like it was jazz coming from a saxophone. She was loving every minute of this session. He was kissing, licking, sucking, and giving that deep stroke just right.

Yet the phone would stop ring, "Go head answer it." Korey said.

"No baby don't stop keep going." Jasmine was in her zone. He was loving the fact she was will to surrender her body to him at the moment. Something was wrong she need to find out what it was.

"No I think you better take the call." He said. She rolled her eye picking up the phone without looking at the caller ID.

"Hello" she knew this shit better be urgent.

"Jasmine get your ass back up to this hospital. Shannon had to go back to surgery. They're keeping a watchful eye on her to make sure they don't need to take her again. Get here now!" Jay hung up heading back to the waiting room.

Jasmine jumped out the bed into her pants with no panties of even time to wash her ass. Korey knew shit had gotten real; he knew a lot of things about his wife. The only thing that can make her move this fast was a family emergency.

"Are the kids okay?" he asked.

"Yeah they're fine, its Shannon. She's not doing well. I have to be there to see what's fully going on," She said.

"Do you want me to come with you?" He asked.

"You can if you want to," She said as she stuffed her feet inside her shoes.

Korey got dressed just as fast as she did. In record time the two were out the door in separate cars heading for the hospital.

Chapter 9

Dizzy was sitting in the VIP of the smoking lounge. Their normal bartender had sent over a box of Cubans and three bottles when he first arrived. When the waiter came over asking for two more bottles he knew something wasn't right.

He knew these boys had their hands in some heavy shit, but out of all the men Dizzy was always the level headed one. He picked up the phone calling Dallas. He couldn't allow this man to drive home after drinking so much.

Kim and Dallas was on the sofa watching The Mack talking shit.

"I would have got down for Goldie you hear me." Kim thought he was one of the coolest dudes in the movie.

"Oh is that right?" Dallas teased her.

"Damn right," She said.

"I want to be ya mama, papa, sister, and friend but you got to believe in me baby. Can you dig it?" Dallas acted like he was Goldie.

"I can dig it baby," They burst out laughing as the phone rang.

"Hello." Dallas was still chuckling.

"Hey Dallas this James owner of the Smoke & Sip Lounge. I am sorry to bother you at you resident at this hour but I got one of your boys down here on his fifth bottle."

"Cut him off I am on my way to get him," Dallas knew this shit would take a huge toll on Zane.

He got off the couch heading to the door. Kim didn't ask where he was going. She was from the old school, and she played her part. That was the problem with most women, they didn't know their place or how to play their part. Yet when you're dealing with a bawss you've got to walk a fine line to stay on team. Rule number one is never ask questions.

Kim got off the couch heading to the bathroom. She ran herself a steaming hot bath with lavender oil and aromatherapy candles. She was in love with the over-sized tub in Dallas's home. She laid a silk robe across the bed. When she got out the tub, the robe and Dallas were the only things she wanted touch her body for the rest of the night.

As the water ran she put on soft jazz, lit candles all over the bed room, and she even called down to house service for champagne, ice, and strawberries. Kim didn't know what caused big daddy to run off, but when he came home she planned to ease his mind. That was Rule number two: Cater to your man, no matter how late he arrives; Leave clue showing him you were waiting up for him. Remember these rules don't apply to average bitches and lame niggas. This is for power couples/king and queen type shit.

Kim lowered her body into the water letting her hand guide to the place she knew that Dallas would kiss later. She could feel the wetness of his lips as she imagined he was there exploring her body with her. Kim fondled her breast with the one hand as her head rested on the tub pillow. She allowed her other hand to walk down her rock hard abs, between her legs, touching her sweet spot.

It didn't take long, before she was full fledge pleasing herself, yet she imagined she was with Dallas. "Oh Dallas baby that's my spot baby," She moaned as if he was giving it to her good and slow. "Yes go deeper daddy," She moaned out more.

Kim was so deep within her zone she had forgotten the house service had brought up her order. That is until she heard a moan that wasn't hers.

"Oh yes play with that pretty pink pussy," the female voice said causing Kim to open her eyes. She saw this beautiful chocolate covered Asian touching herself. She was breath taking. She never could figure out where Dallas finds the women that work for him, most where so beautiful any straight women would be attracted to them.

"I didn't know I had company," Kim said. She pulled her wet body out of the tub, stepping on the plush carpet. Dallas hated when he was a kid that his mother would always say *"Put a towel on the floor so you don't slip and fall."* That was the reason for all his bathrooms having carpet.

The female opens her eyes, "I am sorry, me, got carried away." She still had some of her accent even thought she was African American.

"Who are you?" Kim asked.

She stood up off the bed. She was 5'6 and her body screamed touch me at 34-46-40. This girl was blessed by her cultures. She had

61

honey green eyes and jet black hair. "I am Wen Michelle," She spoke.

"I turned you on I see," Kim ran her hand across her breast. Wen lowered her head in shame. She knew that Dallas wouldn't be happy to find out this is how she behaves when he was away.

"I sorry. I must go," She said.

"I won't tell if you don't," Kim said.

"I won't," Wen smiled.

"When you saw me in the tub, what were you imagining yourself doing to me?" Kim asked.

"Taste you," Wen giggled cover her mouth.

Kim lifted her leg on the chaise she was standing by. "Do you still want to taste me?" Kim asked.

Wen smiled licking her lips dropping to her knees. She kissed the outer lips of Kim's hot pussy. As she kissed them she could feel the sweet nectar leaking out. She wasn't sure of how much time they had because Dallas was unpredictable; she would not waste time.

She parted Kim pussy lips licking the nectar out of her hole. "Oh so sweet, Wen likes," She moaned as she ate Kim pussy.

"Kim likes too baby." Kim grabbed the back of her head grinding her pussy in Wen face. The harder she grinds the deeper Wen let her tongue go. She was loving every drop of Kim's sweet nectar. She played with her own pussy causing her to breathe heavy on Kim's clit. "Wen cummming, Wen Cumming.... oh shit Wen cummmmming," She said with her tongue still inside Kim.

"Oh shit Kim cummmmming tooo you nasty bitch Kim isssss cummmmmmming.'" Kim kicked her off of her and told her to get out.

"You no like Wen?" She felt used.

"I like Wen but I am in love with Dallas," Kim assured her.

"Wen respected that," She was about to walk out the room.

"I will see you again soon," Kim said lowering her body back into the tub.

"I won't tell if you won't," she winked at then smiled.

"I won't," Kim said as she walked out the door.

Kim knew that she was wrong for sleeping with the help, but that bitch was bad; she could let that one slip through her hands. Dallas wasn't no saint hell, and neither was she. They were enjoying the moments of life for now. Sex was one thing; she could share that with anyone. Yet to love will always be reserved for Dallas only.

Kim was feeling good she sipped her wine bopped her head to the music waiting for daddy to return home.

Chapter 10

Dallas pulled up to Smoke and Sip Lounge. He didn't even understand why Zane would leave Shannon at the hospital unattended. Anything could change for the better or worst in a blink of an eye. He knew he would have to teach this boy the rules to love. Not that Dallas was pro at love yet, but he was the master when it came down to women.

He stepped out of the car handing valet the key to his nineteen sixty-four Rolls Royce. That muthafucka was everything. Ebony black, with red leather interior. A very rare, left handed drive Radford Countryman model. It had ninety-two thousand five hundred and forty-eight miles on it from slow riding. Equipped with air condition, power windows, burl wood fascia, and door caps, map light, thermos and water flask, twin rear trays with towels, hangers, vanity mirror case and accouterments, cigar case and trimmer, twin rear cup and bottle, flask with crystal wine/water glasses, fold down mounted writing secretary, picnic folding table with stools and folding with umbrella and folding traveling tools.

This car was a pimp ride for real, Dallas didn't drive it too often yet the smoke lounge was one of the place he came to when was cursing in it. He headed inside the building heading for VIP. He had scanned the parking lot for Zane's car yet he didn't see it. He walked over to their regular section giving the owner James the head nod letting him know he was there. James smiled thinking about the good old day he shared with his ponta. Now he was all alone; Most of his friends were dead and gone. He never settled down or had kids. This lounge and the people in was the only thing keeping him alive.

Dallas looked at Dizzy wondering what the hell he was doing here. He sat down beside him to see how drunk he really was. Dizzy looked at him, "Man what the fuck you doing here? James you didn't have to call this muthafucka. If I am not welcomed here I'll leave this bitch." Dizzy was lit up like a match box.

He tried to stand up and Dallas grabbed him by the shirt snatching him back down to his seat. "Sit the fuck down and watch how you talk to me," Dallas said.

"Man fuck you, I am grown. I don't need you trying to control my personal life. The only reason I allow you to control my business life because the money good. And working for them low down ass pigs didn't get me shit but a dead wife and child." Dizzy was hurting; Dallas thought it was Zane yet hear Dizzy is out of his damn mind.

"You're grown right?" Dallas asked.

"You damn right I am." Dizzy said as he drank another drink. Dallas knew he didn't need it but he wanted so he let him have it.

"Well let's talk about what got you here. I know it could be the loss of your wife and child. I thought you left that hurt in the dungeon when you moved out of it," Dallas stated.

"I did man... I really did," Dizzy said pouring another drink.

"What happened then? How did we get here?" Dallas asked.

"We got here when I allowed myself to fall for that bitch Jasmine," He said.

Dallas knew that Jasmine had something to do with the hurt on his ponta. He knew this relationship shit between the two could end badly since she was married. He didn't think it would happen so soon though. Jasmine was caught up in the lifestyle, yet this was Dizzy's everyday life.

"Man do you have to disrespect her like that?" Dallas never taught his crew to disrespect woman because it didn't take all that to express what you feel.

"I am wrong man, forgive me." Dizzy knew he was drinking too much trying to ease the hurt knowing the pain will never go away. He loves Jasmine so much.

"Forgiven, now talk to me." Dallas was trying to keep him talking until he was ready to go home. He didn't want to force him out causing a scene in such a classy place. Plus, the fact he had too much respect for the owner James to bring drama to his place.

"Man it's like this. I wanted to wake her up with breakfast in bed. Yet when I entered the room to check and see if she was still sleeping she was up getting dressed. My heart knew where she was going, but I still needed to hear her say it so I asked. She told me it was time for her to make things right with her husband.

I know they got kids and all, but I know the nigga don't make her happy like I do you feel me?" Dizzy couldn't believe she did it like that. She didn't stop to think about how he felt. He would have respected it more if she had lied. Yet just like the cold blooded bitch the Duffle Bag Bitches were, she ripped his heart out.

"You're right he will never make her as happy as you. Yet you will never be able to compete with the love and security he has stored away just for her." Dallas knew this fool was thinking with a broken heart instead of his brain.

"How you going to say some shit like that? You're my family nigga, I ain't no lame ass nigga. I always protect the women in life." The moment the words left his mouth a lump formed in his throat.

He felt like shit, "At least I tried too." Dizzy often wondered would he ever be able to share the love he had for his wife and daughter, or would he die alone because he walked on the dark side after losing them.

"I am not saying it like I am a cheerleader. You know I am always for the home team," Dallas assured him.

"Well what the fuck you saying then?" Dizzy asked. Dallas chuckled because his man rarely acted like this. It was hilarious and sad to see his boy like this.

"Let me school you. You started fucking with a woman that's married with four children. She is young but living a mature woman's life. She enters our world and we're wildin, getting money, blowing shit up, living the mile-high life. The both of y'all fucking in crazy places, enjoying life. Nigga that's fun," Dallas told him.

"That's what I am saying. What we had was real." Dizzy smoked his Cuban shaking his head.

"Hold on hear me out," Dallas wanted him to see the whole picture.

"I am stilling nigga," Dizzy assured him wonder how a lame could top him.

"This man married her, he's the father of all four of her beautiful children. Her family loves and respect him. When she chose the streets, he loved the kids the same. Even moved them out of harm's way. Came to the spot willing to risk his life for her, checking me in the process. The icing on the cake is when she came back, he was waiting with open arms. I am sorry fun can't replace love like that," Dallas was on his grown man shit as he schooled his homie.

"Damn you're right about that, I fucked up. I mistook fun for the real thing," Dizzy knew he had better judgement then this.

"Hey baby it happens to the best of us. Let's go home nigga." Dizzy knew that even Dallas the player of the year has had his heart broken before.

"Let's got home," Dizzy staggered as he stood up. Dallas caught him, helping him walk. James smiled as he watched the two stumbling out the door.

Chapter 11

Shannon was stabilizing; the second surgery was good. She was still being watched around the clock. Shannon could tell when someone was in the room with her but she knew to them she wasn't awake. Yet she was or so she thought. She was asking questions she thought they could hear, *"Zane is that you? Where is Jailah? Did my baby make it?"* When she got no response she knew something was wrong.

Her body was in a coma yet her mind wasn't. She knew that she had fucked up by doing the things she did to be lying this bed. Shannon told herself, *"Okay I can't talk. That's not the end of the world, let try this."* She tried to move her hands then feet then she wiggle her whole body from side to side. Yet nothing happened, this is bullshit. *"Aye Jesus I know you hear me because I am not dead. But I am not alive to these folks in here either. I am sorry, I know I've got a hard head. You promised me I was going to be a bride so what the hell is up with this? My bad, I don't mean to yell but you can't be serious right now.*

Let me make it up to you, I can't make it up from this bed though." Shannon was going in but then she thought about Zane.

"Lord better yet, I might need to stay the way I am for a few days. He's going to kill me if I get up. I am praying I didn't take that baby from him. He will never forgive me for this. How is he feeling lord? Angry? Or scared?" Shannon didn't hear response. She didn't know how things would turn out from her yet she felt herself falling off to sleep even though she rather be up.

Korey, Jasmine, and Jay were all sitting around talking when Mack came back from checking on Zane. Jay stood up the moment she saw Mack. "How is he?" She asked.

"He's good. The crazy ass nigga broke his hand when he punched that damn wall," Mack assured them as he looked over at Jasmine with her husband.

"Where is Dizzy?" He asked.

"I am not sure," Jay said.

"I am not talking to you, Jasmine where he is?" He asked.

"I don't know," She rolled her eyes at him.

"Yeah okay, muthafuckas want to act brand new," Mack didn't like the shit she was trying to pull.

"Aye don't start no shit with me Mack," Jasmine was on her feet now. Korey jumped up before Mack could respond.

73

"Let's go outside for some air," He said.

Jay shook her head in Jasmine's direction saying she agreed with the suggestion. Jasmine took the cue. Jay knew that Mack was raw. You never knew what the fuck was going to come out of his mouth. So it was best if she got Korey the hell out of there.

As they walked out Mack asked Jay, "How is she going to play my nigga like that?" He was pissed.

"Your nigga knew what he was dealing with before it came down to this. It's only really four things in the world that can change a person's action. Life, Death, Love, and Money," Jay told him.

"I know that, but Shannon going to be cool man. She's a muthafuckin G, that's my sister in there. She's going to get through this shit. We're built for this," Mack was convinced that Shannon would be fine.

"I know she will too man, we just have to stay strong. Fighting amongst each other isn't going to help," Jay knew that Mack wasn't mad at Jasmine, he was just stressed about the situation.

"Man I ain't trying to fight with ole babe, that my muthafuckin people. Even though she brought that lame ass nigga up in here with her," He said.

"He's family, he was bound to show up." Jay laughed.

"I know. I just though my nigga Dizzy had really found a good one," Mack smiled.

"I understand that," Jay smiled. She knew how he felt. She thought she found a good one in Q, yet people often change.

"Fuck all that! What was it you wanted to speak to me about?" Mack asked her.

"Oh snap! You remember the nigga Cash?" Jay asked him.

"Yeah that fool had the drop on your ass. You were a goner," He laughed.

"Ha ha real funny bitch ass nigga. Check this out though why his niece here? She tried to get the drop on me at the hotel I been staying in," She schooled him a little bit.

"What? Get the fuck out of here. Why the hell are you staying in a hotel?" Mack didn't know what the hell was going on.

"It's a long story on the hotel situation. Look my place is ready for me to move in the bitch, but I got this hoe Mariah tied up to the chair. I got to get her ass up out of there. She stank like hell, I am going to need your help," She told him.

"I am not touching no stanking ass heffas. Why you didn't just kill the bitch?" He didn't know what kind of games Jay was playing by keeping the stanking ass girl alive.

"I couldn't do it there," She said.

Mack looked at her like she had lost her damn mind. He didn't know why she was trying to talk to him like he was boo boo the fool. "Girl quite playing games with me, come with the real," He knew it was more to this.

"Alright I am gone keep it gangsta. I kind of felt bad for leaving the little bitch out in the cold. I know Cash was all she had and I feel like I took that from her," Jay said.

"You didn't take that from her Cash did. All he had to do was get his weight back up. From what I hear he was plugged in with Venom. Yet he fucked that up stalking you," Mack informed her. She knew that Cash was out there bad but not that bad.

"Damn I didn't know all that. This girl is broke, look like she's on drugs, and her child died," Jay said feeling sorry for Mariah's hardship.

"Damn! Did you and this stanking ass girl have a Doctor Phillip moment?" Mack asked. He didn't know were Jay head was at, but she better put an end to this shit.

"Hell no it wasn't nothing like that it just, never minds." Jay's emotions were running wilding, and she was wondering when her time would come. She knew the wages of sin was death. She knew after this last lick that Venom offered she was out for good. There was no amount of money that could drag her in.

"I know what you're going through. I have seen many of my nigga's fight for their lives. Some won the battle, some didn't. That's a part of life. If this job has you living with regrets, then this is not the business for you," Mack told her.

"I am starting to feeling like I am not cut out for this shit anymore," Jay was honest with him.

"I am going to help you with ole girl, but deciding to leave the team is all you. I don't want to see you go," Mack said.

"I am scared Mack," Jay hugged him wondering if Shannon would ever get up.

"We all are," Mack knew Shannon's illness was killing the whole team.

Chapter 12

Zane was outside smoking a blunt when Jasmine and Korey came out. When Jasmine spotted him she walked over to check on him and Korey followed. She knew he wasn't doing well. She didn't even think the man had a bath today. He was so stressed out about Shannon he was forgetting to take care of himself.

"Hey boo," Jasmine said to him.

"I am doing the best I can," He waved. He popped the pills the pharmacy filled for him, then he hit the blunt again. He passed it to Jasmine, and she puffed it remembering Korey was there.

"You remember my husband don't you?" She asked.

"How can you forget the face of a nigga that put a gun to your head?" Zane said knowing that love had changed him. If it wasn't for change Jasmine would be a widow.

"Jasmine I am about to get up out of here and pick up the kids. I will be at the house when you're ready to go," Korey leaned in kissing her forehead and she blushed. He was leaving because his temper was trying to break free. He knew this wasn't the time to lose control.

"Okay baby it won't be too late. I am going to cook dinner," She smiled, and that was music to his ears, he was sick of fast food.

"Thank the lord I got my wife back," He kissed her lips this time before leaving.

Zane watched Korey. He didn't like him, but he respects the love he had for Jasmine and their kids. It was hard to find real young black love. He was proud to see them fighting for each other. "I am glad to see you're back home."

"It feels good to be back, but I've still got to talk to Dizzy. I fucked up, and I didn't leave right. I think I owe him that," Jasmine said.

"Hey I am no love doctor but I thought you and Dizzy were cute together. Yet you and the fool that walked away share old school love. That shit ain't so easy to come by now days," He schooled her.

"I know. I just got caught up in the lifestyle," Jasmine finally admitted.

"Now it's time to get out, the lifestyle got your sister in there fighting for her life. This shit ain't for y'all. This is for street niggas not beautiful woman like y'all," He was speaking from his heart. He knew one thing; If Shannon pulled through, she out this business whether she liked it or not.

"I am agreeing with you, but can we also agree you need to go home bath, sleep, and take your other daughter out to clear your mind," She stated.

"Who's going to be here with my girls?" Zane asked like he was the only person Shannon had.

"Family, my mother, me. She will never be here alone," Jasmine laughed at him.

"Twenty-four hours Jasmine if anything changes good or bad you call me, promise?" He knew his body needed the rest. He also missed Jailah. She needed to see one of them to know she would be okay.

"I promise. I just want you to take care of yourself. You have so many people depending on you. Shannon, Jailah, Lovely, and me," She laughed at the fact he named her niece Lovely. She knew for sure Shannon would hate it, yet she could do nothing about it.

"Oh is that right?" Zane cracked a smile for the second time in 48 hrs.

"You know it," She smiled.

"Let's go inside so one of these fools can drop me off," He didn't have his car he left it at Dallas house.

They entered the hospital and Jay was coming from the direction of Shannon's room. Mack was talking to the girl that helped them the night they brought Shannon in. Jay ran over to them. "What good?"

"We were about to ask you the same thing," Jasmine said.

"I was just checking on her before I get ready to get up out of here. They say her vitals are really strong. They still want to watch her closely because her vitals are up like she's awake yet she's not," Jay smiled at the new she was sharing.

"See I told you she will be fine," Jasmine hit Zane.

"If she wakes up please call me," Zane begged.

"You know it," Jasmine told him.

"You're leaving?" Jay asked.

"Yeah I need the rest," He winked at Jasmine.

"I am about to breakout to once Mack brings his ass on. Who is that bitch he's talking to anyway?" Jay didn't pay attention to her the night she helped them.

"Some bitch Tasha knows," Jasmine said.

"Looks like trouble to me," Zane assured them. They all busted out laughing causing Mack to look their way. He bid the bitch a goodbye heading back to his crew to see what the hell was so funny that Zane was laughing.

"Why y'all up in here acting ghetto laughing all loud and shit," Mack asked like he was the police of happiness.

"Don't come over here with that bullshit, why would you be talking to that bitch?" Jay asked.

"She cool peeps, plus my baby fucks with her," Mack said. He didn't see shit wrong with chopping it up with Candy.

"Watch that bitch man. With a body like that she is not harmless," Zane put him on game. Jasmine hit him for that statement.

Mack laughed, "Bruh I wasn't even thinking about the ass on the bitch. But it is big, I wonder did she pay for it?" They all laughed because that fool was crazy.

Candy watched them laugh and talk shit until the left. She was wondering where Tasha was when Mack first arrived. She finally got the chance to ask him when his home girl left him alone. She didn't understand how Tasha could leave her man around these women. Friends my ass; she saw Jay hugging all up on Mack. Ain't that much hurt muthafuckin world. She wished a bitch would.

While she was talking to Mack she got his number. Told him she was trying to move a little work on the side, and he told her he could put her on in a few months. He had to tie up some loose ends first. She didn't mind because she could tell he was holding. He could set up shop up in her house. All she needed was for him to find his way to her bed.

Chapter 13

Jay followed Mack to his house to park his car. When Mack got in the backseat of Jay's car Zane wondered what was going down, yet he had too much weed to care. He arrived to the house expecting noise but all he got was an eerie silence. A part of him hated he agreed to come home. He was here now, so he turned on the TV and they were identifying the dude from Jay's building as Nicholas Humphry.

When he heard the last name he knew that was West's baby brother. He often wondered what made the girls take him out. He knew it wasn't word on the street because that would have been handled. All he knew was that the nigga was in the ground. Now all he needed was his wife to wake up.

He cooked himself something to eat; hospital food was the worst. He cooked shrimp Alfredo, garlic and herb salmon, with a spinach salad. He even had a glass of red wine. He was halfway through the meal when he thought about how Shannon loved his cooking. Zane wished she was here with him so he could feed her then make love to her.

After thinking about her he was no longer hungry anymore. He cleaned up the mess he'd made, then made his way to his room. He called Shannon's mother to let her know that he would be there to pick up his daughter tomorrow for love. Once he was done he walked into his shower with the seat.

He threw his clothing back out onto the bathroom floor. Then he took a seat on the cold ceramic bench. The water automatically ran down his rock hard body once he spoke his name. It was programmed for him and Shannon. They even had an "Us" setting.

As the water ran down on him, he cried.

"Lord I just want to say this, I never asked you for love. You had never given it to me in all my life, so it wasn't huge on my list. Then one day this woman walks in and I am love sick. I am talking about from the moment she walked in I could hear you say that's her. I told you I didn't want her, yet you wouldn't let up, so I gave in. Now I love her more than I love myself. I don't get you sometimes, I give in, do what you ask yet it's still not good enough. What do you want from me? I will give whatever it is as long as you give her back."

Zane washed his body then got out the shower dripping wet, the hair around his navel laid down like baby hair. He wrapped a towel around the lower half of his body. Then he threw his wet body across the bed praying and cried himself to sleep.

Jay pulled up to the hotel Mack looked at the upscale understanding why she didn't air the bitch out up in here. She could have pulled it off, he was sure the room wasn't in her name. He understood this place was hot as hell. He didn't even really want to go up in that bitch for real.

Jay got out the ride and the valet greeted her. Mack could tell she had been here for a while. They were enjoying the tips she been giving them. As he watched Jay handed the valet a hundred-dollar bill. The man smiled thanking her as he took the key.

He looked Mack up and down, he was impressed with the jewelry that draped his neck and wrist. The jewelry had so many diamonds in it the shit was blinding. The valet was a young black man on his way to college but he knew that Mack had never seen the inside of a college a day in his life. He spoke to Mack before he got in the car. "What you doing for a living? I want to be whatever you are," He smiled hard.

Mack knew it was the way Jay wasted money on the tips, and the jewelry around his neck. "You don't want my job man, this life chose me, and I didn't choose it. You're on the right path. When you graduate from college call me and I will by any car that you want," Mack said.

"Thanks man," The kid held on to the number like it was a lottery ticket. Then he jumped in the car driving away.

As they walked into the hotel heading to the hotel Jay told Mack, "That was some real shit you said to that young man. I hate when older niggas try to teach these youngin that this shit is the way to go." Jay had a new respect for the boy.

"I am not that nigga this shit will get you killed. The nigga that pulled me in killed my homie who was fourteen two weeks after we got down with him," Mack remembered that shit like it was yesterday. He torched the young boy then blew his head off in front of him.

As they enter the elevator Jay asked, "Why'd he do the nigga like that?" She didn't get some people out here.

"A fifty dollar short," Mack said as they stepped out the elevator.

"That's fucked up," Jay said.

"I am sure that shit never happened to me," Mack said as she stopped at the room door.

She asked, "How?" She knew Mack had been in game for a long time.

"I killed him," Mack said with a straight face stepping into the room with her. Jay had to piss, so she cut to the bathroom before going in the bedroom where Mariah was. Mack made his way to the bedroom; He was trying to get this shit over and done with. He knew Jay was soft hearted on this chick but the moment he got her out the hotel, he'd kill her if Jay didn't.

They needed no loose ends coming back to haunt them. Mack entered the room. It stunk like hell. He saw the chair and rope but no Mariah. "Aye Jay," He called.

"Yeah nigga, I am coming I had to piss," She yelled.

"TMI, I thought we was coming to get Mariah stanking ass?" he stated.

"We are," She came out the bathroom wondering what the hell was wrong with this boy. She entered the bed room.

"Where she at?" Mack asked pointing to the chair.

"FUCK!" Jay couldn't believe this shit.

"Fuck is right, you got another problem running around out there. You have no idea when they coming back to collect."

"This bitch had help," Jay picked up the cut rope.

"We've got to get the fuck out of here." Mack told her.

Jay called the front desk for a stat check out demanding they have her car out front when she got there. She informed the manager to charge her for the night and a thousand-dollar tip for the great service they provided.

They exited the room, Jay hit the light as she left. She didn't even bother to take the shit she had there with her none of it was important. Yet she had funny she was overlooking something. They took the steps down to make it to the car faster. "Mack I feel like I am leaving something," She said.

"You can re-buy whatever it is, bring your ass on." He told her. They hopped in the ride jetting off as the same young boy watched them as if they were movie stars.

Jay dropped Mack off and he looked at the worried look on her face. "We will handle what comes behind this. Just don't take your ass back to the room," He told her.

"Thank bruh," She knew he had her back.

Chapter 14

The sun was disrespectful as a muthafucka Dizzy thought as he tried to roll away from the direction of the sun. Then moment he rolled vomit flew out of his mouth like a water hose. He tried to jump out the bed thinking about the 1000 thread count on his sheet set. The vomit kept coming causing him to fall out the bed into the first batch.

He wasn't in the mood for this shit; hell he didn't even remember what the hell he had drunk. He was trying to pull himself off the floor yet the vomit wouldn't stop. He just laid on the floor in it until his body was just heaving.

Dizzy didn't know what the hell was going on with him until he heard a male voice and the click of a gun. "Man what the fuck you doing on the floor?" Dallas releasing the cock on the gun putting in his hip. He tried to help him but slipped down in the vomit with him.

"I was trying to make it to the bathroom," Dizzy said as he laid there.

"Man I know this ain't no got damn vomit?" Dallas was pissed. He had on a thousand dollar pants, and a six-hundred-dollar shirt.

"I am sorry man," Dizzy said lifting his head and throwing up all over him.

"Aye nigga I am going to fucking kill you." Dallas was losing his mind; he didn't love this nigga this much. He couldn't believe this shit was happening. He knew he should have taken his ass home, but no he wanted to be a good friend. Look what being a good friend gets you. Sitting in vomit, fucking up thousand dollars in clothing.

"Oh my bad I will pay for the outfit son," Dizzy knew how Dallas was about his clothing.

"I know the hell you will," Dallas pulled himself off the floor. Yet he drew his gun again when he heard footsteps.

When Tequila entered the room, she saw the man with the man holding a gun. She dropped the food she was carrying. Throwing her hands up, "Don't hurt me" She said wondering what the hell she had walked in on. Dizzy was still laying on the floor she didn't know if he was dead or alive.

Dallas was wondering who the fuck this lady was. "Dizzy who the hell is this lady?" He didn't know this nigga had women with kids to his house.

He rolled over on his back. "That's the manager of the building," He said.

"Ma'am why are you coming up in this house as if you live here?" Dallas still had the gun on her.

"I just wanted to surprise him with breakfast because he was so nice to me yesterday," She said.

"Note to self, don't surprise a gangsta because you might fuck around and lose your life," Dallas told her.

"I am sorry," Tequila said. She was scared out of her mind. Yet her pussy was on fire from the excitement.

Dallas lowered the gun. "Go over there and help him to the shower," He said. She was more than willing and Dizzy didn't have the energy to fight with her today.

She walked over, "Coming on baby." She didn't care what was on him she just wanted him in her arms.

"Be careful I got throw up all over me," Dizzy informed her like that mattered.

"That alright. Let's get you all cleaned up," Tequila said.

Dallas could tell this woman had been waiting for this moment. He could also tell that Dizzy wasn't feeling her like that, but he would settle today. He would make sure he didn't get stuck on a bitch he really doesn't want. Although he could use her company for now.

He watched her walked him into the bathroom. The water ran and he could tell she was helping him undress. Dallas called out to him, "Bruh you good?" He was just checking.

"Yeah I am straight baby," He assured him.

"Alright I am about to head home. Call me later, and don't forget to bring my fit money," He teased but was serious.

"I got you G," Dizzy yelled.

"I am gone," Dallas yelled heading to the front door.

Tequila made sure he was stable in the shower before leaving him alone. He had a hell of a hangover. She cleaned up the room for him with the cleaner she found under his bathroom cabinet. She stripped the bed putting fresh lining on, putting the sheets in the washer.

As she was about to mop the floor he called her name. "Tequila baby I need a dry towel," He said. She smiled feeling like she was his woman for real.

She handed him the towel telling him "Your clothing is on the sofa. I am still cleaning you room. You just get dressed and relax."

The shower made him feel better. He was coming back to himself but still felt a little sick. "Thanks I appreciate your help," He really meant that.

"You know I don't mind," She said as he sat on the couch getting dress in gray basketball shorts and tank top.

Jasmine had called Korey telling me she was leaving the hospital. She told him she would be home, but she had to make a stop. Then she was in for the day she need to rest. She was glad she could let Zane get rest. Her mother told her he had her niece with him. Zane took her to lunch and to get a build a bear then he would come the hospital to give her back to Shannon's mother.

As Jasmine drove in her car she called Dizzy but the phone was going straight to voicemail. That wasn't like him, she was worried about him. Even though she was the one deciding to end this she needed closure. She continued to call him while she was in route to his house. Jasmine knew he probably wasn't feeling seeing her. This was the last time she would creep off to end things the right way. Dizzy was chilling on the couch thinking about how much he drank last night. That shit was insane, he had never drank that much in his life. Tequila had his crib smelling good from all the cleaning she had done for him. He knew she wasn't the one for him, yet she was good woman. He had to admit it felt good to have a woman around. That was a part of his life he would fix when they get back from this trip.

Tequila came into the living rooming wearing one of his tank tops. That thing was hugging her body like oh my god. She had her hair pulled up in a messy bun because she had washed it. "I hope you don't mind be borrowing your shit until my clothing get dry. I can't go back to the office like that." She said sitting down in a chair across from him. He had a beautiful view of her trimmed pussy.

"Nah I don't mind it at all." He had to clear his throat to keep from drooling. That pussy was sitting up so right it screamed come taste me. He didn't want to know this bitch like that. Sometime he hated being a man because that dick real had a mind of his on.

She acted like she didn't know she was turning him on. "What the hell did you drink last night?" She shivered thinking about the stinky shit she cleaned up.

"Man all I remember was bottles," He burst out laughing. She laughed with him. He realized she had a sexy smile. "Come here," He said before knew it.

"Me?" She pointed to herself.

He got up off the couch crawled over to her. He entered his finger into her pussy without asking. He could tell he was welcomed by how her pussy was dripping into his hand as he worked his finger in and out.

"Waitttttt," She said as he lifted her shirt sucking her nipples.

"I I I I wantttt mooorrrre than justttttt…" She was cumming. He knew it because her body was shaking uncontrollably.

"You want what?" He picked her up placing her up against the wall. He slipped that ten inches deep up in her.

She yelled out, "Ommmmmggg it's huge."

He laughed. "I am still waiting for you to tell me what you want." He was fucking her with that long stroke. The pussy was grade A too, but he just knew this bitch was gone be too much to deal with. Even though he knew she was a headache waiting to happen he knew he was going to fuck her again. He didn't understand why crazy women had the best pussy. "I Hmmmm wantttt alllll of yooooooouu." She screamed while he was biting her neck and fucking her brains out. This shit was better that she imagined it would be.

"This is all I have to give now," He wasn't going to lie to her. It was up to her if she wanted to fuck with him.

"Okkkkay OMGGGGGGGGGGGG just keep fucking me," She begged causing him to go harder. His dick was jumping hard like it wanted to let that nut go, but he wasn't ready to cum yet. He bent her over the couch pounding that pussy to death.

"Oh Daddy Oh Daddy, please don't stop fucking me," She screamed as he held her bun knocking her back out.

Jasmine pulled in the parking lot spotting his car. She knew that he was home, she wondered what the hell was going on with his phone. She'd been calling the whole way over she couldn't get through. She got out the car and passed the leasing office. They had a sign on the door reading Late Start Day. It said something about the office opening at noon.

She was glad the bitch was gone. Every time she would come the bitch would have the blinds in the office open watching her as she went to Dizzy place. Jasmine hoped the bitch choked on her lunch and died. She knew the bitch had something to do with her car catching fire. When she can prove it she was going to whoop the bitch.

Jasmine looked at her watch as she climbed the steps. She didn't want to be out too long. She wanted to see her babies and chill with her family for the rest of the day. She got to the door, and she was about to knock when she heard voices on the other side of the door. She looked at the door knowing she could tell it wasn't locked the key hole was turned. Real criminals have special eyes for shit like that.

"Throw that pussy back, throw it back girl, make this dick cum baby," Dizzy was ready to let the nut flow, but he held it so long it wasn't trying to come.

"Fuck me in my ass." Tequila was so turned on she would have let him cum in her nose if he wanted to.

"Oh shit I am cumming bitch I'm cumming." He pulled out busting all up her back and in her hair. "Argggggghhhhhhh take that shit," He said laughing.

"You so nasty," She said.

Jasmine stepped in the apartment, "Yes the fuck he is." She was disgusted he was up in here fucking this bitch.

He looked at her wondering what the hell she was doing there. He pulled his pants up while Tequila ran off to the bedroom. She didn't want Jasmine to beat her up. When she locked herself in his bedroom he just shook his head.

"What's up Jasmine?" He sat on the couch lighting one of his pre rolled blunts.

"What's up is what you ask me and you up in here fucking this bitch," Jasmine said. Her feeling was hurt.

"Girl you're out your muthafuckin mind. You stood in my house told me you had to fix your family. Now you're standing in my house acting like you hurting that I'm fucking in my own house," Dizzy couldn't believe this shit.

"I have been gone twenty-four hours, damn you couldn't wait could you?" Jasmine didn't expect to walk in on this. Most of all she didn't think it would hurt this bad.

"How long have you been married? Cause I've been single for years now," He was being an asshole.

"Fuck you Dizzy I came here to apologize for ending things. This is bigger than me and you. I have kids and history with this man. I am sorry for letting things get out of hand. Yet I see I meant nothing to you for you to move on so fast," She said.

"I was dating that woman when I started fucking with you. I put her on the back burner because I thought what we had was real. Until I was told this wasn't what you wanted a couple days ago.

Forgive me for not sitting around waiting for you to come back to me. I have wasted enough of my life already," He was speaking of the years he grieved his loss.

Tequila came out the room. "I am sorry to interrupt; I need to leave to open the office." She buttoned her shirt as she eased past Jasmine to the door.

"Baby call me later," Dizzy said blowing her a kiss. Jasmine was pissed to the max. She was about to speak but Dizzy cut her off.

"Jasmine I love you, but I love me more. I am coming second best to nothing. I will never ask you to choose your family over me. Please don't ask me to wait around in case you have a change of heart. The one reason you're here has to be for closure. If that's what it is Jasmine be happy, love your husband. Me, I am going to enjoy life until I find some to share what you two have already found. Let yourself out. I am going to take a nap," Dizzy walked into the bedroom smoking his blunt.

Chapter 15

Mariah woke up in the bed under warm covers. She thought she was dreaming. She jumped up out the bed turning the light on and realized she was in a huge hotel suite. She was scared Jay was fucking with her mind. Mariah crept out the bed room into a living room. There was a man sitting on the couch.

He felt her presence "Look who's finally awake," The voice said to her. It sounded so familiar it was scary. Cash would always say that to her when she was a kids. Yet the man sitting on the couch wasn't Cash.

"Who are you? Why I am I here?" She asked.

"Come on Riah sit down let me talk to you," The strange face familiar voice said.

"Okay now this shits creepy, kill me now or I am leaving. I have been strapped to a chair for days. Now I am talking to a stranger that sound like my uncle. I can't with this shit no more." Mariah was heading for the door. She felt like she was losing her damn mind.

"Stop Mariah hear me out please out," Que begged.

"Why? I don't even know you! I appreciate you helping me get away from the heartless bitch Jay. I don't know what she was waiting for to kill me. I am sorry I am not taking any chance I am getting the hell out of here." Mariah didn't mean to be rude, but she was over this shit. It was time to change her life for the better now that she had a second chance.

"Mariah it's me Boo bear." Que aka Cash said.

Mariah was halfway to the door in a robe and no shoes. Upon hearing the name, she couldn't stop the tears from fall as she turned around to see if he was serious. She knew no one in the world outside of family knew that name. "Are you serious? Why? Why did you leave me out here alone? I thought you was killed. The body and face were disfigured but the driving license on him was you." She didn't know what the hell was going on. She didn't know people in the street went through shit like this.

"I didn't leave you I sent money every month, I couldn't return once my man's got killed. We did the face off. I had him laying on Jay for me but when I was listening to everything taking place between her and him. I realize she didn't love me like I love her. I changed my identity to offer her a life of freedom from the bullshit. Yet she was heartless, and I gave the signal for him to kill her." Que needed a drink. He wasn't ready to deal with all of this.

He had been watching Jay since she had been in the hotel. He knew why she shook the spot she had. Jay was always once step of the game. Once he put her on game with Nick B. He realized he had spoken to soon when she stopped talking his call. Then a week later the nigga was found dead in her crib. A part of Cash wanted to be mad at her slick ass. Yet her criminal mind had Cash hooked on her. The last night she left he broke into her room. He was shocked to find Mariah tied to a chair.

He sipped his drink wishing he could just let the love for Jay go. It was an obsession, and he planned to have her by any means necessary.

Mariah was lost for words because she received no money. "I didn't get any money for you or anyone," She assured him.

"I was sending it to the apartment I got you and the baby before I left." He wasn't sure how she didn't get the five thousand a week. He'd sent it for the last two years. Nothing was ever returned to him.

Mariah sighed sliding down wall to the floor. She sat there with her head down. "After you left I allowed Tory to move in with me. I figured since you weren't around to stop me. It was a bad idea; he took over the whole place. Friends slanging dope out the house, bitches running in and out. All of this caused CPS to come take my baby. After I went to court they told me what to do to get the baby back.

I went home to tell him he had to clean up his act or go. He was in my place with a bitch fucking. Yet I was the one that got locked up because I didn't know the fool filed a restraining order on me," She was crying hard now.

"Mariah you can't be that fucking stupid can you?" He was pissed. He was going to put out a hit on that little nigga.

"Do you still love Jay? That's why you here right? You stumble on me stalking her." Mariah wanted him to know how easy it was to be stupid in a world where you feel that person is all you've got.

"I have been dating her as she knows me as Q. I dropped a bomb on her that caused her to go in hiding. I proposed to her last year she declined. I would reveal who I was to her after we were married," He must be honest with himself and her. Mariah shook her head laughing "See how easy love can cause us to be stupid. The question is doing we live the rest of our lives in stupidity or do we take our lives back?" She had fire in her eyes, she wanted Jay head on a platter.

"You are a mother now I will handle Jay. I know she doesn't love me, or any man. Jay is all about self, I am in love with the most selfish bitch in the world," He threw his glass against the wall. "She has taken everything from me but I will not allow you to lose your child behind this," He assured her.

"He's dead Cash." Mariah said staring out in space. No matter what he believes Jay took everything she had to live for. Now she wanted it back.

"What?" He couldn't believe his ears.

"Yes he was ill," She said no longer crying.

"I am sorry, I never meant for this to happen to you. I don't know how we got here," Q sat on the couch.

"I do the bitch Jay; she doesn't love you. She never has, and never will. I'm going to kill her even if I have to kill you to do it," Mariah wanted him to know how serious she was.

"I know she doesn't, and I understand where you're at. If we do this, we've got to plan well. The crew she runs with is official," He needed Mariah to know what she was up against.

"I am ready for whatever but I need to eat first," She was hungry as hell.

Q laughed his ass off as he called room service.

Chapter 16

Jay's new place was 1.8 acres of mature landscaping & flowering garden. This mini estate is the view of the vista. It's a center piece for the surrounding homes. It features ten feet hand painted Trompe l'oeil walls. Custom moldings, wood & marble elegance flooring carried throughout the kitchen/breakfast room.

An adjoining sunroom and family room. The master suite was designed from The Ritz in Paris. Barrel vaulted ceilings, marble flooring, dressing area with his/ her walk-in closets. The second floor offers three bedrooms with two private bathrooms. A sitting room with fireplace and study area. Finished with rec room, office, additional bedroom and two more bathrooms.

The backyard had a resort like setting. Brick patios with wrought iron fencing. A court yard formal patio which overlooks the pool and lush rear yard. This place was everything she dreamed of and more. The six thousand dollars a month price tag was a steal for her.

As Jay sat in her kitchen she couldn't shake the fact Mariah was on the loose. It had been two weeks and three days since her and

Mack discovered the little bitch was gone. Jay wanted to know who the hell helped her. Whomever it was, is laying for her. She couldn't could pinpoint who, Cash was dead, and the nigga with the casino. She chuckled thinking about the fruit roll up in Manhattan gunning for her.

It was time to make another move in a few days. Jay knew this was her last run, and as much as she loves this house she might just leave this whole country behind and move to a foreign country to rebuild her life.

Shannon had been in the hospital for a week and some change. She was breathing on her own, yet she still wasn't out of the coma. The doctors didn't understand because her brain activity, vital signs, and breathing was great. Her beautiful baby love was three pounds now. Everything was looking great, she just needed to wake up. She knew that Zane was there every night. He would go home in the morning bath, rest, and hang out with Jailah.

Her mother had just left the room to meet Zane out front. They never bring Jailah back to see her in the condition she was in. Shannon had been awake since midnight she never opened her eyes or moved. She wanted no one to know she was awake. Zane came in she was facing him. Her mother would position her toward the door every morning.

She didn't allow the nurses to come in and out all night. Shannon's mother had been in nursing for the past twenty years. If she could do it for strangers, she damn sure could for her child. Shannon was blessed to have the family she had. Zane came in and he was still sleepy. Jailah had wanted to stay up watching Frozen. He had to sing all the songs with her until she fell asleep.

He kissed Shannon good morning on the lips as always. He could have sworn she kissed him back. Zane shook his head because he knew he was tripping. He was about to sit down in the chair when he heard, "I know my breath stank, but you don't have to act like that," She said in a muffled tone.

Once he heard her voice he missed the chair falling on his ass. Shannon giggled softly. Her throat was sore from the removal of the tubes and not speaking for so long. Zane hopped up off the floor to the bed. "Shannon," He was shaking her now.

"Boy stop shaking me I am not that damn well yet." She was still feisty; he was glad she was back.

"I need to inform the nurse." He said.

"No not yet. They're just going to start poking all over a bitch. I want to know how you are," She asked.

"Scared, angry, hurt and now happy. Before you I was never scared of shit. When I got angry I end what causes it. I didn't understand the mean of hurt feelings. The only thing that use to make me happy was money. You changed all that, I appreciate you for that. I can't do this if you're going to risk what I am dying to be for you. I can't handle losing you to the streets. You want to know how I feel there it is. It's time for you to choose," Zane need her to understand his pain and frustration.

"I am sorry I didn't mean to do this to you. I have more money than I know what to do with. I have a king that will never let me struggle. I promise I am out. It's going to be hard for me knowing you play in traffic and I am not out there to cover you. As your queen I respect the terms you have set before me. Now I only ask one thing what is my daughter's name?" She knew in her heart she was alive.

"Her name is Lovely." He smiled.

"Oh god you didn't," Shannon hated it but loved it at the same time.

"Now can I inform these people you're awake so we can get my family out of here?" He was over excited. Tears weren't needed; He had cried enough, and it was time to rejoice and be thankful.

"Yes baby," She loved this man.

He kissed her heading out the room. He stopped before he got the nurse station. *"Thank you man for coming through. I am going to try to repay you by loving her the right way. I won't become a saint overnight but I'll never forget that I owe you."* Zane was so grateful the man above heard his cry.

The nurses were running their mouth about the Have and the Have Not's. "Girl I couldn't believe Kathrine hit that hoe in the head," They slapped fives.

"I know I was like bitch die," The second nurse said.

A third nurse jumped in, "I am going to have to check this show out." The first one was about to speak when Zane said, "Excuse me ladies I hate to interrupt your conversation." The first nurse looked at his fine ass.

"Baby interrupt me anytime," She adjusted her breast.

He rubbed his bread licking his lips laughing "My wife in 403 is woke," He stated.

"Oh my god is she." The second nurse took off because that was her patient.

"Can you tell her I am going to make a few calls while you do what you need to do?" He asked as she was hauling ass.

"Yeah I got you love." She didn't want to hear shit from the doctor. She couldn't afford another write up this month.

Zane took a seat in the waiting area across from the nurses calling Dallas.

Kim was sitting in Dallas office with her bags by chair. She was about to head back to her world and she couldn't wait to retired in six months. She will be free to play with Dallas whenever he wanted her. He was smiling at her "Baby what time your flight leaves?" He asked.

"In two hours." The driver came in to get her bags and inform her the car was ready whenever she was.

"Damn I going to miss you, come sit on daddy lap," He said.

Kim straddle him kissing him passionately. He pussy became wet; she couldn't get enough this man. "Damn I want you," She said.

"I wish I was the only thing you wanted," He said. She stood up looking at him wondering what the hell was talking about.

"What the fuck you on?" She rolled her eyes.

"This." He pointed to the video of her and Wen getting it in.

"Damn I am sorry I tasted your candy. I was bored, you had business to tend too. Plus, as you see she started it not me," Kim was kicking herself. She should have known this bitch had cameras in his home. He didn't trust no damn body.

"Kim when you come to my house treat it respect. Never take anything I didn't give to you," He told her.

"I said I am sorry," She pouted.

"Come here," She leaned in and he kissed her.

"I love your spoiled ass now get out," He gave he a nose kiss this time.

"Love you too daddy," She knew when she pouted he would give in. This man was everything she needed and wanted in her life.

He could help to laugh at her; she was hell on wheels. None the less, she was his, and it was time for him to focus more on enjoying life instead of making money.

Chapter 17

Dallas's phone rang; it was Zane, "My nigga talks to me."
Zane could tell he was in a good mood. He'd heard Kim's fine ass
was in town.

"I see Kim is keeping you happy," He said to him.

"Me and my damn maid," Dallas said.

"What?" Zane didn't know what type of shit they were on.

"Never mind that, what's going on with you?" He could hear
life in Zane's voice.

"My wife is awake; my baby is gaining weight; I am a
blessed man." He was cloud nine.

"Aww man that's some beautiful shit right there. I'm happy
for you man. Is there anything you need me to do?" Dallas didn't
want to rush up to the hospital just yet. He was going to let her gain
strength.

"I do need one thing from you," Zane had a serious tone.

"Say the word it's done man." Zane was his lifelong friend.
He would do anything in the world for him.

"My wife no longer works for you. I don't want my woman
in this field. I want her home taking care of my children, shopping,

traveling etc. I just want her to enjoy life, I will handle the life threating jobs," Zane knew he would understand.

"I never knew bringing these women in would shake my crew up so much but it has. The power love doesn't follow rules. Neither does my crew. I respect you man, your wife and your rules," Dallas assured him.

"Thanks man that means a lot to me. Can you call the crew letting them know she woke?" Zane asked.

"Now you want me to be your damn secretary," Dallas shook his head.

"It's not like that man," Zane laughed.

"I got you family," He hung up with him calling Jay.

Zane was so happy he skipped down the hall to see his baby daughter Lovely.

Dallas called everyone letting them know what was going on. Jay thought he was calling about the business trip. When she heard the news about Shannon she hung up on Dallas call Jasmine immediately. They agreed to meet up at the hospital. Jasmine was loving being back with her family. She still needed to holler at Jay about what went down at Dizzy's place. She didn't expect to walk in on that. They even called Tasha to tell her the good news. She was excited.

Tasha was overjoyed Shannon had pulled through. She was going to the hospital to see her. It had been three weeks since the shit with ole boy went down. Mack wasn't home. She called his phone, but he didn't pick up. She was sick of this shit. Tasha didn't know what Mack was on but he had her fucked up. She wasn't going to stay a sitting duck.

Tasha grabbed her car keys heading out the door.

Mack looked at the missed call. Tasha had called again. He was down in the hood but he picked up the phone calling her back. "Hello," she answered.

"Kill the attitude," Mack couldn't stand this snappy attitude this baby was giving her.

"It's dead what you want?" She asked driving.

"Are you driving?" he asked.

"Yes I am. My sister woke up and I am going to see here. I am not staying in that house no more. You running around out here,

119

but think I am going to stay put. Not happening another day boo," She was in rear form.

It was turning Mack on, he would let her know. "Girl I will slap…" the phone hung up in his ear. He tried to call her back, but she didn't pick up because she wasn't in the mood for that bullshit he was talking. Tasha didn't know what was going on him lately. She would not worry about it today. She would find out in due time.

"Fuck, get off of me," Mack said to Candy. He'd been fucking her for the last week. He didn't mean to fuck her. He'd came over to bring her the work to see how she wobbled. When he got there she had on these shorts that allowed half of her juicy ass cheeks to hang out the bottom. They handled the business, then smoked a blunt. As he was facing the blunt she dropped down sucking his dick. He wanted to stop her, but that girl had the grapefruit head game. She sucked the life out of him.

At first he was coming for the head. Until the day she let him knock the lining out the pussy. He missed hardcore sex; he loved wild style sex. Tasha couldn't do that at the moment. He slipped up fucked her wildly until she stopped him. He knew he needed to break this shit off with Candy.

"Damn why you mad at me cause that bitch acting stupid," Candy said.

Mack grabbed her by the neck, "Do you like living?" He asked.

"Sometimes," She was a sarcastic asshole.

"Bitch act like it," He said releasing her.

"Fuck me," She knew he got mad whenever she mentioned Tasha or disrespected her.

"You sick and I've got to go," He tried to pull his pants up. She dropped down to her knees sucking his dick as she smoked a blunt.

"Arrrrghhhh shit girl, that's not going to work this time. It's a family matter boo," He said as he was fucking her face like it was a pussy. He didn't think this bitch had a brain in her head.

"Boy give me this nut damn." She handed him the blunt. He didn't know every blunt she rolled blunt was laced with work. She was a hustler that dipped in the pack from time to time. Not enough to fuck with her money but just enough to release the freak all night long.

Mack inhaled the smoke allowing his head to fallback. He was dying to cum, so he could get back to his crew. Yet something about this whole set up had him hooked. He loved Tasha with all his heart and he wanted Candy to know that. "You will never replace her if that's your goal. We can end this now," He handed her the blunt.

She released his dick from the grips of her lips. "I am not trying to replace her as long as I can make a little and get the dick. I am straight. She can have the heartache." Candy went back to pleasing him.

"She's got the whole," He said. His mind was screaming to get the hell out of there while his body was greedily enjoying every moment.

Mack knew Tasha was mad as hell with him due to his behavior this past week. He would make it up to her someway, somehow. He looked down at Candy sucking him like her life depended on it. He vowed to himself this was his last time fucking Candy. He prayed Tasha could forgive him.

Chapter 18

Beverley Hills, Ca was the place to be. Everything was live and all the who's who were there. Vicious loved it but Venom wasn't accustomed to it yet even though she'd been there for many years, even raised a child. He was turning into a man. Medallion better known as Mellow in his younger days was determined to name their son king of what they have built over the years.

Venom didn't think he was cut out for the shit. That was the main reason she called her sister asking her out to lunch. She wanted to talk to her about this alone. No interruptions; she needed her point of view to be heard. Better yet, she needed to know how to deal with this situation.

The car service pulled up on Rodeo Dr. in front the Beverly Hills Hotel. The driver parked and exited the car to open her door. Vicious stepped out the car in a black close-fit dress crafted from English-woven Cluny lace structured, gathering at the bodice complements by the sweetheart neckline.

A fitted waist with dart tucks and a back split at the skirt completed the feminine silhouette. The design was fully lined in a soft silk. Matching pumps and clutch compliment of Burberry. She was killing shit; no woman would believe she was the mother of a teenager.

Venom was waiting in The Cabana Café. She looked at her Cartier watch a few times. She hated when her sister was late. She watched as she sashayed in like she owned the world and everything in it. As she took her seat Venom said, "You're late."

"As if time stand still for me." Vicious was a class act as always.

"Bitch I am not for this high class shit today," Venom assured her.

"Well bitch next time invite me to your muthafuckin backyard not Rodeo Dr. hoe," Vicious came alive.

"That's more like it and my backyard is the shit excuse you," Venom didn't play about her yard.

The waiter made his way over to the table. "Are you ready to order madams?" The women came there often, and he knew them well.

"Yes we are love. I will have the Truffle Fontina Eggs Benedict with an English muffin, Canadian bacon. Poached eggs to die for. With Citrus One the combination of cucumber, pineapple, lemon coconut H2O, and Aloe Vera." This drink makes you jog in six inch heels. Vicious loved this place.

"And you my love?" He looked at Venom.

"Stuffed French Toast was maple syrup, mascarpone, and berry compote." It was a sweet treat you could have in the morning. "With Extreme Toffee Coffee sweet, buttery toffee paired with a hint of chocolate and mountain grown coffee," She smiled. Venom loved the sugar high this meal gave.

"Coming right away." He hurried off.

"You know I love these fancy ass places yet you hate them so what's the reason we're here?" Vicious was hoping it had nothing to do with the job her crew was handling this weekend. She couldn't hold off on this thing any longer.

"It's about Young Mello taking over soon. I know the little nigga not built for these streets. He's a fucking rich kid for crying out loud. Yet Medallion has him brain washed and hyped to do this. I am trying to respect his gangsta yet he doesn't have a gangsta bone in his body. My baby is going to get killed out there," Venom was tripping hard.

"I agree with everything you're saying but Medallion has been grooming him for this all his life. Now it's time to let him prove himself. I know it's hard to hear that from me knowing I would never allow my daughter to enter the game. Somehow it's different for men. It's an ego thing." Vicious felt her sister's pain, but this was one thing she was going to have to gamble with.

"I have Mack coming on a Capo because Dallas is shutting down shop." Venom wasn't happy about the closing but she understood he was ready to enjoy life. No one wanted to die doing this line of work.

"That's great, that nigga is a warrior. You really have no worries with him there. Mack isn't a fuck up when it comes to the street. He was born to do this." Vicious knew this kid all too well. She remembered when she whooped his little ass for hustling in front of her trap. He was freaked out because he thought she was the same woman that hired him to work there.

"Yeah he is. It took me a while to track that little nigga back down. He had changed his name and everything. He was spooked; He still is today," Venom laughed.

"Sis we've been doing this shit a long time. I wanted the power when I first started all this. Some days I wish I never got into the game," Vicious had to be honest about it all.

"I am moving back home," Venom dropped the bomb on her.

"It's like that?" Vicious asked.

"I will need to be close to my son, he also needs to see the world he's about to walk into. Saint Louis is no Beverly Hills. He needs to know what he is up against. I am sorry but this place never grew on me anyway," Venom laid all her cards on the table.

"Black isn't going to be happy about this," Vicious didn't know how the fuck she would make this shit work.

"What the hell does this have to do with Black?" Venom was confused with her sister's statement.

"If you're going home I am too." Vicious loved this place, but she loved her sister more.

"I can't have you uprooting your family for me," Venom said.

"Why are you in Beverly Hills Aja?" Vicious hit her with the government name.

"Because you moved her Asia," She said.

"My point exactly, bitch we ride together, grind together, and we going to die together. We were separated once in our life and that will never happen again. Plus, it would be nice to spend time with Lil Rob and Mrs. Brown's old ass," Vicious laughed.

"Yeah ain't nothing like family," Venom said.

They enjoyed their food making small talk, laughing about the past. Wondering how much the hood really had changed. Venom was so happy her sister was going back home with her she took her on a ten-thousand-dollar shopping spree on Rodeo Drive. The spree didn't last long.

Chapter 19

Q had moved out of the little suite and into a nice two bedrooms for him and Mariah. He could tell that Mariah wasn't the doe eyed kid he'd left behind. She was cold and dark. She had cut her hair into this funky body, black with purples tips. She even got tattoo of her son on her back, golds, and a lip piercing. The girl looked good, but he knew this wasn't her normal swag. She was taking on the swag of Saint Louis women which he hated because they were too cocky.

Mariah was coming from her room when a knock at the door caused her to jump. She was still leery of her surroundings since she didn't know if Jay was still looking for her or not. She kept a heat in her room just in case. She wasn't putting all her trust in no one anymore. Not even Q a.k.a Cash. This sick love he had for Jay could cause him to turn on her.

Q came from his bedroom opening the door. He slapped five with the handsome man. He was caramel, six feet, one hundred eighty pounds, and green eyes. He smiled at Mariah. He had never seen her before. Her mocha skin and phatty were calling him but business comes first.

"What's good man?" Que asked.

"Aye everything thing man," Roc told him.

"What you got for me?" Que asked him.

Roc hand him pictures of Jay at her new house. She had even bought a new Aston Martin. He even had pictures of Dallas and Kim making love, Shannon awake in the hospital with Zane and her daughter, Mack with Candy shopping, Jasmine with her husband and kids, and Tasha and her big belly. He was watching the whole crew just as Q asked.

"Damn you got growth, love, drama, and new life," Q was impressed with his skills. Roc worked for Dallas, so he knew the nigga was more than capable of getting the information he needed. That was how he could keep an eye on Jay's ass. Roc's been helping him for some time now.

"Man you know how this crew gets down," Roc assured him.

"I see they live well." Q was pissed because his shitty life was a far cry from this shit here. Mariah was listening to all the information Roc was giving Q. She was taking mental note to put a plan in motion.

"I've got bad news," Roc said.

"What is it?" Roc asked.

"They're shutting down the camp after they leave for this next run. It's over. They're ready to live normal lives," Roc said. He was only down with Dallas for the money. When Que came to him for information on the crew he was more than glad to make the extra. He needed all the money he could get. He was greedy; this line of work made people act this way some times.

"Normal lives? Ain't that a bitch! They go around fucking up folk's lives, but they get to go on living normal lives?" Mariah was pissed.

"Calm down we're going to handle this," Q said to her.

"You could have dead this shit a long time ago," Mariah would not act like he couldn't have handled this by now. Roc loved the fire that danced in her eyes.

"I am not about to play the blame game. I can't change what's done. I am trying to fix this shit now Mariah," He knew she was angry.

"About fucking time," She went to her room slamming the door. She didn't want to hear shit unless it involved wiping out the whole team.

"I am sorry about that man back to business," Q said.

"It's all good. She must have lost a lot being this mad," Roc was interested knowing more about Mariah.

"Yeah she has. When is this move is supposed to go down?" Q need facts so he could get the ball rolling.

"The crews leaving in two days, I am sure they won't be in California more than forty-eight hours. That's how they operate, so you will be able to snoop about Jay's place. I suggest you stay low because the place is every upscale and at any signs of bullshit the laws will be all over you. I don't think you will find much. If you want I can pay her a visit leaving a few bugs in the place," Roc assured him.

"Yeah man that will work, I don't want to out myself before I even get started," Q said.

"Whatever plan you come up with don't try to make it up close nor personal. You will be dead before the shit is even in motion. These are not rookies you're dealing with," Roc was trying to put this nigga on game. He didn't understand why the nigga didn't just let the shit go.

"I got you. Thanks for everything man. You're going on the trip with them as well right?" Q asked.

"No I got a team on standby out them ways," Roc told him.

"I see you got it going on man," Q gave him dap.

"I got a little something shaking." Roc was being modest since he had been down with Dallas he had stepped up a recuse crew in several cities from Saint Louis to Huston. He was getting money it just wasn't enough.

"That's what it do if you have some free time you should call my niece. Take her out somewhere nice, help her clear her mind." Que knew he was checking for her, he wanted to give Mariah a reason to smile.

"Are you sure you cool with this? Cause I am grown ass man dog. That likes to do grown man shit, you feel me?" Roc wanted the nigga to understand if she will, he was fucking.

"Man she's a grown ass woman as well, just don't play no games with her," Q didn't want her hurt again.

"I am not going to lie and say I have never hurt a woman before. I will say this; I am willing to be honest with her about what I have to offer. It's up to her where this goes from there," Roc schooled him.

"I respect that. It was good seeing you player," Q shook his hand as he walked to the door.

Chapter 20

Tasha didn't know what the fuck had been going on with Mack. He didn't even make it to the hospital to see his sister. This was so unlike him, family always come first. Tasha had spoken to Jay last night to see if she had heard from him. She hadn't, and she even called his street brothers Dallas and Dizzy. No one knew shit. She didn't know if they all was playing games with her but the shit was about to come to an end.

Tasha was pregnant as hell, so if Mack thought she was going to allow him to do whatever the hell he wanted to her then he had another muthafuckin thing coming. She had been calling his phone since she woke up getting no answer. She couldn't deal with the drama when she first woke up because she had a doctor's appointment to find out the sex of her baby. She was hurt he wasn't there with her to share this moment.

Tasha thanked the nurse at the clinic as she gave her the information for her next visit. She was twenty-eight weeks. This was almost over; her baby would be her. She'd planned for her child to be raised a two parent home because she wasn't, but the way things were going she wasn't sure any more. She loved Mack, but she didn't know if he still felt the same about her.

Tasha got in her Range Rover and bent a few corners to see if she could find this nigga's car or him hanging in the hood. He had been telling her since he was becoming Capo soon he need the streets to know who he is. She bought that shit for a few days. She was over the shit now. It was more than the hood who knew his damn name. Tasha hadn't been in the hood over a year. She had no reason to travel down this way that was the reason Candy was shocked to see her.

She had been driving for about thirty minutes. Yet she'd seen no signs of Mack. She was pissed. She was getting hungry, so she was about to head home. As she was passing the projects she stopped by Candy place to see what she been up too. She knew it wasn't much cause this hoe was still in the slums. The girls just wouldn't leave. They gave her section-8 and the bitch still wouldn't leave that low income housing complex.

Tasha pulled up low and behold Mack's car was parked out there. She couldn't believe this nigga was hanging out down here like this. Tasha stepped out the ride. She was in her black and pink

Jordan joggers, matching T-shirt, and Retro J's. She was on her pretty girl shit, with her inches blowing in the wind as she walked across lot headed to Candy's place.

She didn't see Mack hanging out now, she knew if anyone in the hood knew what was going on it was Candy. She heard her name called causing her to stop. It was her homie Bowleg. She hadn't seen him in a minute. He walked up to her.

"I thought that was your ass that hopped out the range. What you been up to besides popping that thang?" He rubbed her belly.

"I ain't been up to nothing. I've been chilling for real, getting ready for my baby to get here," She said looking at Mack car.

"I am glad you're doing well shit you know a nigga still out in the bricks; can't wait to get the hell up out of here. Just waiting on the right plug to come along you feel me?" He was a petty hustler, but he was loyal and dedicated. He just needed someone to give him a chance.

"It looks like some nigga out here getting some money," She pointed to Mack's car to see what the hood had to say.

"Awe that's some nigga that Candy been fucking with. She says he going to put her on then she going to have the hood on fleek getting that money. You know I don't trust the bitch like that," Bowleg said not realizing what the fuck he just said.

"Oh is that right? Walk with me over to Candy's crib," She said like she was on some nosey shit.

"Let go," He threw air punches at her. He liked Tasha because even though she was stacked up right she never used her body to get men. Nor did she ever act stuck up. She was really the home girl.

When they reached the door Tasha asked, "B knock for me?" She was looking around her purse.

Candy heard the knock asking, "Who is it?"

"Bowleg," He said.

She didn't know what the hell he wanted, so she opened the door trying to down play him. "Nigga what you want? I keep telling your broke ass the shop ain't open yet. I am in here with a boss, I need you to respect that," She said wondering who the girl was with him. She had her back turn.

"My bad I was just bringing Tasha.... *Zingggggg*" The sound caused Bowleg to stop what he was saying. As he watched Candy's body hit the floor. Mack heard a bump, so he came to the front to see what the hell was going on. When he saw Candy he looked up at Bowleg he asked. "What the hell happened to her?" Before Bowleg could speak Tasha got to swinging on his ass. Bowleg didn't know what all this shit was about but he didn't want Tasha to harm that baby she was just bragging about over no hood shit.

The neighbors came out with their camera phones and shit as Bowleg was pulling Tasha off Mack. "Hold on baby girl," He said. By this time Candy was woke, and she jumped up.

"Bitch I know you didn't tase me." She ran up like she was about to swing.

"Hold on don't do that," Mack grabbed her hand.

Bowleg was still holding Tasha when Mack walked up to her. "I am sorry, for real," He said.

"Sorry my muthafuckin ass you been over her hanging out with this cum guzzling bitch!" Tasha was hot.

"You damn right he was, bitch you mad because the nigga ain't been home in a while. I was guzzling all his cum. While he knocking this pussy and asshole out," Candy didn't have no class rising her dress showing her pussy.

"That's the kind of nasty bitch you want? I am done nigga you will never see my son. Bitch you dead believe that, you fucked up my family, and you gone pay. I hope you ain't been smoking blunts with the hoe because she smokes primos." Tasha walked off to her car. She would not let the hood see her cry. Bowleg followed her to make sure she was cool.

Candy walked back in her house, "Fuck that bitch she not trying to see me." She twerked her ass showing her pussy from the back to the whole hood.

Mack couldn't believe this shit as he slammed her front door. Gathering up his belongings he couldn't believe he missed finding out the sex of his child. Now Tasha was saying he couldn't see the baby. He was going to have to make this shit right.

"I just got two questions, did you bate me because you saw how Tasha was on at the hospital? And do you smoke primos?" Mack was pissed to think that he had touched that shit. This bitch was trying to make him an addict.

"Yup I only smoke primos. Why you think this pussy stay wet, and that dick been beyond hard? I saw you loving all up on Tasha that night. I knew then you fucked with hood bitches. I made

140

my move. Shit I like nice shit too, can I get a Range Rover too?" She laughed.

Before her knew it he knocked her clean the fuck out. "I like hood bitches with good hearts," He stepped over the low bitch heading to his car. He didn't know how in the fuck to make this right, but he knew who did. Dallas.

Chapter 21

Shannon was doing great, and she was even sitting up now. Zane couldn't be happier, his baby had even jumped up to four pounds. It was a blessing that his family was doing well. Lately he had been spending time between both rooms. He even brought Jailah up there a few times. She was glad her mom was feeling better. He took her to see Lovely; she was so happy to be a big sister.

He knew the time was coming to head out with the crew. Dallas had given him a pass to fallback. He was planning to take the offer, staying with his family. He entered the room with Shannon. She was watching Maury. "You live for drama," He laughed.

"Hey baby come here let me holler at you." She was going home tomorrow but the baby still had to stay a little longer. That was fine with her since she could come see her anytime she liked.

"What's good with it girl?" He laid all over her like she wasn't in a hospital bed.

"You're so damn crazy, I need you to be serious," She kissed him.

"Okay talk to me," He said.

"I know I am coming home tomorrow; I know you guy are supposed to leave out the night." She said.

"I am not going." He assured.

"I know that but I think you should. The guys need you out there. Don't worry about me I am fine. I will be her waiting and making wedding plans for when you get back." Shannon was making this wedding happen in the next thirty days. She had lost the chances too many times, not this time.

"Baby I don't want to leave you behind. I am out the game. I am ready to buy a house and live life," He told her.

"I respect whatever you want to do. These guys will be lost without your help. I know you don't want your family to be a part of this, but you can't forget the people that caused you to find this happiness for you." That was the realest thing anyone could have said to him. He knew it was from her heart.

"I will think about it baby," He assured her.

"That's all I ask," Her phone rang as he kissed her.

"Damn I knew I shouldn't have brought that thing up here." He said handing it to her before hopping in the chair and turning the station to ESPN.

It was Tasha, and she was crying like a baby. "Calm down sis I don't know what you're saying." Zane looked her wondering what the hell was going on. Shannon hunched her shoulders trying to find out.

"Mack was cheating with this nasty bitch I know named Candy," She said.

"How does he know her?" she asked.

"He meet the bitch the night we brought you in. She knew he was my man, and the bitch smokes primos. I think he been doing it with her since he hadn't been home in days." Tasha was crying and packing her shit. She was checking into a hotel for the night. She would look for a new place tomorrow.

"Girl are you fucking serious? Where is he now?" "I don't know. I tased that hoe and left. I am packing my shit. I am out this bitch. I am sorry to call stressing you out. You're still in the damn hospital, what I am I thinking?" Tasha's head was all over the place. "It's okay Tasha. Please call me when you make it to the hotel." Shannon felt bad for her. She didn't know what the hell was wrong with that boy.

"I promise I will. Again I am sorry to bother you," She was still crying hard as she hung up. That wasn't safe for the baby to be stressed out.

"What the fuck is going on?" Zane asked. He heard how Tasha was crying.

"Mack done lost his damn mind," Shannon said. She was wondering if that's why she had seen every one but him.

Zane stood up out his chair, "I know that fool ain't putting his hands on that girl is he?" Zane didn't like men putting their hands on women. That was hoe ass shit to him. He felt if you've got to whoop your woman's ass to keep her in line you should just leave her alone. But Mack slapped the bitch to sleep.

"No, he was cheating with some girl named Candy. Tasha said he's been missing for days and she found him at the bitches' house. She even said the bitch even does primos." Shannon didn't know what the hell Mack had gotten himself into.

"What the fuck? I knew that bitch was gone be trouble." Zane could believe his man was moving like this. "Where is he now?" Zane asked. He needed to holler at that nigga.

"Tasha tased the bitch and left him in the apartment with her. She doesn't know where he is, but she's at the house packing her shit and heading to a hotel." Shannon was worried about Mack hoping this woman didn't have him hooked on that stuff.

"This shit is crazy," Zane couldn't believe this shit. This nigga was out here on this bullshit knowing it was time to handle business soon.

"Yes it but you have to find him. You can't leave him out there alone," She loved that fool just as much as Tasha did if not more.

"I will baby. I will," He assured.

"Where do you think he could be?" Shannon asked.

"A fuck up this bad, he's at Dallas place." Zane knew when shit got real, the crew ran to Dallas for advice.

"Go. Call me when you find him." He stopped to look at her and smile. Then hurried out the door. He loved her more each day because of the love and compassion she had for people even in her time of need.

Shannon wanted to know who this bitch Candy was. She buzzed the nurse to come in at once. "Ms. Shannon you need me?" She was the sweet nurse; just what Shannon ordered.

"Have you seen my cousin Candy I meant…?" She cut Shannon off just as Shannon wanted her to.

"Candice Jackson? I know her from the hood. I didn't know that was your people. She be wilding. Girl I hear she had beef at her crib today. I was mad I was at work, she called in. She will be back tomorrow morning." She ran down all the tea.

"Damn my family still turnt up while I am up in here. I can't wait to get out this place tomorrow," Shannon was excited.

"Is that all you needed?" She asked.

"Yeah love, sorry to bother you," Shannon apologized for wasting her time.

"Girl you good. I love patients like you," She said walking out the door.

Shannon got on the phone calling the hospital complaint line. "This is Rita how may I assist you?" She was chipper as hell for this time of evening.

"I am patient in your hospital. I want to make a complaint about one of your employees," She informed her.

"I am sorry that you're having an issue with one of our staff members. Will you please state your claim?" She needed to put all this information into the computer system.

"I hate to say this but she smelled of weed, yet it seems to me she was high on something much more," Shannon stated.

"This is a disgrace to the company's name. What is the person's full name?" She knew this report had to go out ASAP. Anyone accused of using drugs must be drugged test before clocking in on their next schedule day.

"Candice Jackson," Shannon said.

"I am sending the report in now ma'am and sorry for your inconvenience. Please allow us to send you up a few things from the gift shop. No need to tell me the room number, all in house calls show. As asked your name will not go on the report." She assured Shannon.

"Thank you so much," Shannon was cool with that. They had nice shit in the gift shop.

"Enjoy your stay and get well soon," She ended the call.

The bitch wanted to play dirty, but she didn't know who she was fucking with. Tasha was a Duffle Bag Bitch by all means and they protected their own. This hoe was supposed to be Tasha's friend. She violated by fucking with her man. The job wasn't the only thing the bitch was about to lose.

Shannon jumped on the horn calling Jay.

Chapter 22

Shannon put Jay up on game about what happened. Then Jay called Jasmine on the three way. "So that's how the bitch moves?" Jasmine asked. She didn't like muthafuckas trying to fuck with people close to a muthafucka. She felt it was too many people in the world to be doing some fucked up shit like that. She beat bitches about hers. "Yeah that's how the bitch rolls." Shannon said.

"How we gone handle this, cause this bitch got to pay for it." This was no lay down shit. They needed bitches in hood to know how the game was.

"She going to lose her job tomorrow morning for sure," Shannon informed them of what she done.

"Let's handle this shit when we get back from Cali. Talk to Tasha and see what she wants do about this shit. Crying will not make Mack or that bitch understand this shit is not a game," Jay stated.

"I can do that," Shannon assured them.

"Then it's on," Jasmine and Jay chimed in ending the call.

Dizzy was sitting back in his polo pajamas telling Dallas about how he was pounding Tequila's back out then Jasmine busting up in the bitch. Dallas couldn't believe that shit.

"Nigga no?" He was laughing hard.

"Nigga yes. I was out fucking done but catch this."

"What?" Dallas knew it was shit in the game.

"She was mad like she didn't just cut shit off with me. Talking about I couldn't wait to bring a bitch off in there," Dizzy still didn't believe the shit when he was saying it.

"You know women be tripping out like that," Dallas told him.

"I don't know what the hell she wants from me but I am not about to play these games. I have wasted a lot of my life feeling sorry for something I had no control of. I am not about to allow no one to put me in a box at this point in my life. I love Jasmine, but if that nigga makes her happy I am all for it. I don't want to stand in the way by any means," Dizzy meant every word that left his mouth. He didn't have no hard feelings for her.

"Boss shit my nigga. I am glad you bounced back. You had me scared for a minute," Dallas said.

"Nigga I should be whooping your ass, you left the damn door unlock. You know the Duffle Bag Bitches raw. She could have killed me in that muthafucka," He laughed but was dead ass serious. The girls will take a muthafucka life fast.

"You right about that, but I am not apologizing. While I was getting your drunk ass from the Smoke and Sip Lounge my bitch was here fucking my maid," Dallas said. When he first checked the tape he couldn't believe these hoes. All up in his home freaking; disrespectful ass heffa's.

"Nigga stop lying," Dizzy said.

"If I wasn't catching feelings for Kim I would show you," Dallas couldn't put his baby on blast like that. Nigga didn't share videos every day, but you can bet it wasn't their main chick. Just something they hitting.

"I can respect that, love looks good on you," Zane felt it was time for his boy to be happy.

"Go on with that shit," Dallas said, yet he really appreciated these guys. He didn't want to live life without them in it.

Mack bust in the recreation room where the men was chilling Wen followed him in. His head was all fucked up he couldn't believe that he played himself like this, most of all hurting Tasha like that. Dallas looked at the wild eye dancing in his head. He knew that look all too well. The boy was higher than heaven.

"Dallas I fucked up," Mack said sweating hard.

"Yes you have, sit down." Dallas order Wen to bring a glass of milk and two Tylenol. He'd never known Mack to do more than smoke a blunt so he didn't know what the hell was going on with him at this moment.

As Mack sat he spoke, "I didn't do this on purpose nigga. I started fucking with that bitch Candy from the hospital. I had been missing for a few days. Tasha came looking for me and she tased the bitch then left. She said the bitch smoked primos. Then she left yelling I will never see my son. I am having a son that I can't see. That shit ain't right man." He was up on his feet again pacing the floor. Dizzy felt bad for him he hated for bitches to bring a nigga down like that. He hoped Tasha uses her crew to make that bitch pay.

Wen came in with the things Dallas asked for and she handed them to Mack. "I don't want no damn milk and shit. I need you to help me fix this shit D," Mack said waving Wen off she stood there confused.

"Drink the shit Mack now," Dallas raised his voice standing to his feet. Mack would take the shit even if he had to force it down his throat himself.

"Alright I will take the shit," He grabbed the glass popping the pills. At that moment Zane walked in. Mack handed the glass back to Wen, and she exited the room.

"I knew you would be here. I told you that bitch was trouble," Zane said.

"I know man. I asked the bitch was what Tasha said true, and she admitted to lacing the weed like she didn't know who the fuck I was. I knocked that bitch smooth out then left," Mack said.

"I don't know who the fuck you are," Zane said. He was pissed with this nigga allowing a low level bitch to play him like this.

"Nigga what the fuck you mean? I'm from the streets. Every muthafucka know how I go," Mack jumped in his face. He wasn't mad at Zane, he was mad at himself and Zane's words hurt his feelings.

"Nigga you don't want these muthafuckin problems for real." Zane never thought he would see the day he wanted to put hands on his right hand man but today was that day.

"Chill out for real, fighting not going to fix this shit. We're family and we have to stick together. We've all been dealing with some crazy shit over the past few weeks but that's life. Especially ours, we can't change what has been done but we can rebuild from where we are," Dizzy wasn't in the mood for no bullshit. These guys were all he had for now. He would not watch it all fall apart.

"Dizzy's right we're family. Where is Tasha Mack?"

"I don't know she not answering my calls."

"She's in a hotel. I don't know which one but she told Shannon she was checking into one for the night," Zane hated to tell him that.

"See Dallas she's done with me man, damn I fucked up," He was hurting. He felt so damn stupid.

"You will get her back," Dallas assured him.

"How man? How?" He fell to the floor crying. All his life he wanted to be loved, now that he had someone willing to do it he didn't know how to treat them. Mack was just used to a life full of madness. Yet he was tired and ready for a change.

Zane pulled him up hugging him, "Man it's going to be alright." He knew how his man was feeling right now.

Chapter 23

Candy came in to work that morning like life was just sweet. She still couldn't believe that hoe tased her, then the nigga knocked her out. He was going to pay for that shit. She didn't know why he was tripping all hard, she does that shit all the time and she was still looking good she told herself as she stood in the bathroom mirror of the hospital taking a picture of herself. She posted the picture on Facebook with the caption, *"Bitch still getting these coins."*

She headed to the time clock hoping today wasn't a long day. When she got there she saw one of the head mangers standing by the clock. She knew then that the day was going to be longer than she thought. Candy couldn't stand their petty asses. They were always watching people clock in and trying to see if a muthafucka was getting extra time. She didn't have time for the bullshit today. She didn't need their extras, she got her shit on the side in the streets or the sheets.

The moment she was about to swiped her card to clock in the manager standing there said, "Candice can you come with me before starting your shift?" She knew damn well they wasn't trying to fire her about calling off yesterday. She hadn't called off in months.

As they entered the office the manger closed the door then walked over to her desk taking a seat. "Candice have a seat."

Candy sat, "What is about?" She asked.

"It has been brought to our attention that you are using drugs," She said.

"What? This is some bullshit. I am not using drugs," Candice was lying with a straight face. She knew that hitting ass bitch Tasha was behind this and she couldn't wait to see that hoe. She didn't play about her money, wasn't no nigga that important. Tasha was trying to act brand new. She knew hoes in the hood shared niggas all the time.

"That's great since we've never had any issue with you since we hired you," The manager said.

"I try to do my best. I don't know who would stoop so low to play with my livelihood," She just knew she was in the clear.

"Unfortunately I can't allow you to clock in without taking a drug test. This company takes these type of things very serious," She hated to do this. She liked Candice's work ethic, but it was her job. She had to follow the orders given to her.

"A drug test? Are you serious? I wasn't even tested when I first got hired. Now that someone filed a report you want to drop me," Candy wasn't ready for this shit. If she had a heads up she would have flushed her system and passed on the primo she had this morning. That shit gave her the energy she needed to keep going throughout the day.

"I am sorry you but have to do it," The manager didn't understand the issue if she was clean. "I am not checking for marijuana," She knew these young girls smoked weed. She wanted her to be clear; she didn't care about weed. She enjoyed a joint or two in her day.

"I don't do shit, but I am not about to allow you to accuse me of this because I am black. All these white nurses you got up in here popping pills like they tic tac's. I am out of here; you will be hearing from my lawyer," Candy stood up to leave. She was pissed just thinking about how hard it would be to find a new job.

"Baby girl don't use the race card because I have a fine ass black husband and two beautiful mixed children. Race is not the issue here. We both know you're hiding something much deeper. Have a good day Candice," She smiled at her as she stormed out there, but Candice had a point. Who else was getting high in there? She jumped on the phone asking for an order to issue random drug tests today.

Shannon was sitting in the lobby. She had been discharged, but she was hanging around to visit her baby, but she was having test ran. From the looks of the bitch coming up the hall cursing and acting ghetto she knew this had to be Candice. Shannon smiled as she was exited out the door. She called Jay, "She's on the move."

"Good. Everything's in motion. Jasmine and Tasha are at the other location," Jay said.

Candice stormed out of the place. She couldn't believe this shit happened to her today. She didn't know what the hell she was going to do. She only had five thousand in her savings. That would not hold her over for long. Her habit ran her a thousand dollars a week. Then she liked to be on fleek that was easily two hundred a week. She didn't even have a nigga holding in the pocket right now because she flaked on them when she was fucking with Mack.

She hit the chirp on her car thinking she would call that nigga Mack and make shit right with him. ***"BOOM"*** was all she heard causing her to hit the ground. Everyone in the hospital heard it causing them to run outside to see if anyone was hurt. Shannon didn't budge from her seat, she watched Jay leave the scene driving slowly as Candy laid on the ground.

The male nurse helped her up. "Candice are you okay," He asked.

She could barely hear him, "I am good. Get off me." She wiggled away from him running close as she could to the car engulfed in flames. Candice couldn't believe that her car fucking exploded like that. She became scared thinking about how she hadn't been out the car for a good thirty minutes. Tasha was playing dirty, and she was going to call her people when she made it home.

The sirens from the fire trucks and police cars were closing in. Candy prepared herself for a long line of questioning she didn't have the answers to.

The fire was out; the car had a bomb that had been place in the bottom of the car on the driver's side. The police informed her that someone was trying to kill her. The bomb was set to go off two ways; the chirp or the startup of the car. Candy's car had a keyless start that automatically turned on her car when she hit the locks to open the door.

She was grateful that she was always stuntin using the chirp. Today that bitch saved her life. This had been a long fucking day for her. All she wanted to want get in the house roll a fat primo, bath, and play with her pussy until she fell asleep.

Jasmine was sitting in the car when Tasha came back saying the coast was clear. Tasha had Bowleg take the two women that live on the opposite sides of Candy apartment out to dinner with theirs. She even gave him money to put them up in a hotel for the night. Shannon had called informing them Candy was heading their way in a cab.

Jasmine's car was parked on the far end of the complex. They exited the car to have a clear view of was about to take place. When the cab approached the complex he turned in to drop her off. Tasha was shocked the cab turned up in here. He must have a heat, and most cab drivers wasn't fucking around.

Candy hopped out the cab spotting a note on her door. She knew damn well it wasn't about no rent because she paid that little shit up yearly. That's why she never planned to leave this bitch until the day she died. She read the note, *"You Fucked the Wrong Bitch Man."* She snatched that shit off her door. She was sick of Tasha's little games already. The bitch will get over it someday. Hell she already got her fried and blew up her car. The nigga threw dick well, but it wasn't worth the headache it comes with.

She stepped into her house hitting the light switch. ***"BOOM"*** The whole place exploded with Candy in it.

Bowleg arrived just in time to see the ladies drive away as the place went up in flames. He looked at the two families, "I can put y'all up in a hotel for the night if you like?" The women smiled, and the children cheered. All he could do was shake his head while thinking, "Them bitches a cold piece of work." Tasha told him she would call him too for housing for the women.

Chapter 24

Shannon was sitting on the couch in her apartment the next morning. She was glad to be home. She was eating bacon, cheese eggs, and waffles compliments of chef Zane. He loved to spoil his queens. Jailah was chewing on her bacon as she watched television when Zane rolled in with a duffle bag. Shannon smiled, she was on the phone with Tasha. "Bitch call me when you get home," She said as Zane sat down next to her asking, "You enjoy your food?" He laid his head on her shoulder.

"I am looking like, are you heading somewhere?" She smiled.

"I know this amazing woman. She taught me no matter what to ride for my family at all times," He said.

"She sounds smart," Shannon laughed as breaking news came across the television screen.

"Sorry to interrupt your regular programming. We have updates on the car that exploded yesterday in the hospital parking lot. The owner of the car Candice Jackson was found dead in the LaSalle Park Projects. The home exploded at the flick of a light switch in the home. Taking out the two apartments next to it. Luckily

those families where not home. The police are still investigating

these incidents yet there are no leads. Again sorry for the

interruption, Mike Wheeler. Fox 2 News bringing you updates first.

"Damn that's crazy," Shannon said.

"It sure in the hell is," He said knowing damn well they did this. These were smooth bitches. He looked at her strange.

"What?" Shannon knew he wanted answer.

"Jay accidently got bomb happy, and we didn't have any place to put them. We called Tasha, and she said she knew the perfect location for them. End of the story, case closed." She filled her mouth with eggs.

"Y'all going to hell." He got up and kissed Jailah before heading out the door to meet up with the guys. He was looking forward to checking out California.

"The bitch gone save our seats for us," She said. He chuckled as the door slammed behind him.

Jasmine kissed her kids sending them off to play. She was dressed in all white with jeans with slits in the leg, a white half shirt, classic visetos high-top cognac, matching weekender visetos, and beige diamonds and stud's sunglasses by MCM. She was fly. She had to look good heading out to finally meet the great Venom. She wasn't about sell herself short. She was going out with a bang.

Korey was in the living room playing Madden 2K. He glanced up at her, checking her swag. "Are you ready to put this all behind you?" He wanted her to be happy. Sometimes the things supposed to make us happy doesn't. It doesn't mean doubt yourself, it means you jump into something without figuring out how you desire to spend your life.

"I am ready. I haven't been as happy as I have been in the past few weeks. I thank you for standing behind me in all this madness. I know it wasn't easy. I also know most men would have never waited. I honor you for that baby," She kissed him.

"Moved out the way. You gone mess up my score," Korey said but deep down inside he was jumping for joy behind the words she shared.

"Well bye then," Just like she was out the door.

Jay pulled up to Dallas's house and hopped out the ride. She had the inches flowing with her Gucci shades, matching t-shirt and pumps. She keeps her heels on high. She was in love with heels. She walked up in the building and the men were buzzing about something they had seen on the news.

"What the hell is the fuss about people?" she asked. They had realized she had entered the room.

"You thick as hell and have on heels yet you can still enter a room without making a sound," Dallas didn't understand that.

"I am a thief in the night," She blew a kissed at him. Causing him to roll his eyes.

"Well thief this shit the news was speaking about got y'all name written all over it," Dizzy said. "I ain't signed my muthafucka name nowhere. So I don't know what you mean," Jay stood on hers.

"Me either," Jasmine said as the room checked her out. She was most definitely killing shit.

"Looks like the husband keeping you happy," Dizzy said.

"He is," She smiled smacking her ass.

"Well the next you decide to visit, call first instead busting in when I am getting it in," He teased.

"Nigga fuck you," She laughed.

He got up hugging her, "Now tell us why y'all handled ole girl like that." Dizzy had his arms around her and Jay.

"Awe shit group picture," Zane dropped his bag jumping in as Mack flicked up a few pictures. He had a beautiful crew.

"We didn't handle anyone," Jasmine said.

"That's not what I was told," Zane said not spilling the tea his wife gave him.

"I don't know what you talking about," Jay said.

"Me either," Jasmine said.

"Well since we not gone get the truth, we might as well get ready to head on out this bitch," Dallas had gotten word from Roc the jet was fueled and ready to roll.

The crew agreed as they all grabbed their bags heading the jet. Mack was glad all the shit was behind him. He was gone do what he had to when he got back to make it up to Tasha. He was the last one to leave the rec room. He pulled the door close as he left. He walked down the hall "Mack," The voice caused him to stop in his tracks. He closed eye praying that god had already fixed this for him.

"Yeah baby," He turned around.

"I am not letting you off easy, but I can't let you get on that jet without telling you I love you. It's been so many times you almost didn't make it back. I want you to know you hurt me, no matter the wrong you do, I will forever love you." Tasha knew she loved this man too much but she couldn't help it.

He grabbed her, "I am sorry baby I mean really sorry. I got caught up in some dumb shit. I never meant to disrespect you like that. I am not saying I am going to be perfect, but I am going to try my best." He assured her.

"The next time you think about sleeping with a bitch claiming to be my friend, you're going to explode with her. You feel me?" She wanted him to know she was from the gutta too yet she wanted to live a classy lifestyle.

"I love you too," He took off running toward the jet. He knew Tasha meant what she said.

Chapter 25

Roc waited for Jay to leave before sneaking into her house to plant the bugs for Q. He couldn't be long because he had to get back to making sure the jet was chartered and ready to roll. Q had asked him if he wanted to make extra money by helping take them out. Roc declined since he didn't have beef with Dallas or his crew. His greed was causing him to go this far. He needed no more sins to pay for come judgement day. He had enough of his own.

The crew was gone as Roc headed to his car calling Mariah. They'd been talking for a few days. He was trying to get her to come out with him but she didn't trust him because of his close connection with Jay's team. He tried to convince her he wasn't part of the team like she assumed. He was just a hired rescues united.

That was the truth yet if the crew every found out he was crossing them he was dead ass. Mariah picked up the phone sounding half sleep at seven in the evening. "Hello," she mumbled.

"Damn girl you in the bed already," He wasn't use to chicks like her. He was used to bitches that get knock down, and jump back up swinging left and right. I guess that was the difference between mid-west and southern women.

"Not yet, just lying around. Ain't nothing much to do." She didn't like this place. She couldn't wait to leave, but she wasn't going back home either. That was still an up in the air type of thing.

"That's what I am saying. Let me take you out for a bite to eat or something?" He liked her little sexy ass. He knew with the situation it would be hard to make her his. He was going to enjoy her for the time being if she ever allowed him to.

"Where are you trying to take me?" She was bored and hungry. Plus, he was good looking. He never pressed the issue on her coming like her baby father use to by telling her she was acting like a little girl.

"I know this dope place called Al's Restaurant. The food a little pricey but its slamming. You don't have to worry about money, anything you want is on me," He said.

Mariah never had a man outside of her uncle Cash willingly spend money on her. "I don't have get dressed up all fancy or nothing do I?" She wasn't in to all of that.

"You don't have to do anything you don't want to baby. I am close by or do you need more time?" He asked.

"Nah I am fresh out the tub pull up on me, but don't come inside." She didn't want Q a.k.a Cash in her mix he had already given this man her number.

"Alright, I will be there in fifteen minutes," He was glad she said yes.

"Perfect," She ended the call hopping out the bed in her bra and panties to find her clothing.

Roc check his face in the mirror as he pulled up on her. His lining was still on fleek. He was always fresh. Grown man or street, he could handle either way. Today he had on smoked grey drop crotch polo joggers, a black v neck polo tee; it hugged his muscular body just right. Hell if he was a girl he would date his damn self. He texts Mariah, *"Outside."*

She texts back *"On my way down."* She was digging this little situation. Mariah was no label girl even though she grew up around hustlers but she didn't fall into the trend. She just liked to look nice, and that wasn't hard with her petite body. She had on a red tank top dress the held tight to all her little curves. Her hair cut was still on point. She threw on some red low top chucks, hoop ears, and a white cross body purse. She was hood cute.

When she got in the car Roc peeped her swag. "You look pretty," He said.

"I am not one of them fancy girls, so if you use to hair weave down to the booty and long fake nails, you not gone get it over here," She informed him.

"No for real, that's why I am feeling this look you got. A lot of times it doesn't take all that. Women be all over dressed just to have lunch with a nigga," He was serious about that, shit like that got on his last nerves.

"You crazy," She laughed as he pulled away from the curb.

"Let's go eat," He sped off in traffic causing her the buckle her seat belt.

Chapter 26

The sun was shining like a muthafucka in Beverly Hills like a muthafucka. The place looked exotic to them. As the jet was landing they could see two limos waiting for them to arrive. Mack love being on the jet sipping champagne and talking shit. He felt it was well deserved when you know it's a chance you may never come back from this. There was something about this hit, it may get hectic he hoped not.

The jet landed and Dallas was the first one off the plane. He got into the car that would take him to Venom's residence. The crew got in the other heading to the hotel. They had to get settled in as always then wait for details on the next move to make. The time flies by so fast they never get to enjoy the cities they visited. That came with the game; had to lay low. Now that it was coming to an end, all of them had plans to see different parts of the world. The limos pulled off two ways heading to their destination.

The limo pulled on Sunset Boulevard, the in center of Beverly Hills, Ca. at the Beverly Hills Hotel. Jasmine dreamed of seeing this place someday when she used to watch the movie *"Pretty*

Woman." She imagined all the Hollywood stars who have enjoyed the timeless glamour of this dramatically beautiful place. It had the relaxed resort feeling.

The crew was speechless stepping out the limo. This place was doper than they imagined. The hotel is surrounded by twelve acres of lush, tropical gardens and exotic flowers. As they walked through the door they could see the famous Polo Lounge restaurant. That was the place to be. There was also Bar Nineteen12 with live music and spectacular views of the colorful California sunsets.

Remaining faithful to the original architecture and interior design, the hotel has been carefully renovated to preserve its supreme level of comfort and flair.

"This place is the shit," Jay said. She couldn't contain it anymore as they walked to their suites. Everyone was in a suite. They passed palm-tree lined pools, complete with private cabanas, refreshing complimentary poolside mini ice-cream sundaes, and mojito pop treats. There was also the Cabana Café. When Jasmine saw the Beverly Hills Hotel Spa by La Prairie she was said, "This fucking place is huge with too much shit in it." She was still waiting to see her room.

"I bet we won't get bored waiting for the details of this case," Dizzy said thinking about one of the message therapists rubbing him down giving him a happy ending.

"Boy shut up you just thinking of freaking in the Spa," Jasmine said while everyone laughed.

"Girl gone, you don't know me like that," She fucked him up reading his mind. He didn't like that shit.

Jasmine and Jay finally made it to their rooms. Each had Beverly Hills Suites next door to each other. It's a modern with a hint of vintage glamour. Oak furniture with touches of mohair and leather. This was the essence of the best luxury five-star hotels in LA.

Featuring the beautiful view, a separate living room with a 42" HD LCD television, and gourmet mini bar. The bedroom had a king-size bed and the luxurious marble bathroom had a shower and a Jacuzzi. Jay wasn't wild about being back in a hotel. She had been laying low in one back home too long. Jasmine lay right across the huge bed.

The guys all were a floor up from the girls in the Sunset Suite. The California style luxury suite has a large private patio with garden views. The spacious sitting room has a piano. In the separate bedroom a king-size bed. The marble bathroom has a shower and a Jacuzzi. Just a few minor changes from the girls but equally great. The men got settled in their rooms calling the woman they had back home to check in. Dizzy even called Tequila.

When Dallas was riding through the residential part of Beverly Hills, all he could think about was how much these houses cost to be this damn ugly on the outside. They arrived to 1400 Coleridge Dr. Beverly Hills, CA 90210. Dallas didn't like the outside of this one either as the driver opened his door.

Venom had been waiting for her best friend to arrive. Dallas might have made the cut of her husband had she never waste time on Sean. Through it all he has hung in there with her. He hated when she moved here. In this business he didn't get leisure time to travel unless it was business related. The moment she saw him pull up she shot to the front door.

She jumped in his arms, "I am so glad you made it. How's the team?" She held him tight.

"They're good, getting settled in." He said. She was about to speak when a male cut her off.

"What I tell you about hugging on strange men all the time?" Medallion asked.

Dallas couldn't believe how much he'd changed. The nigga was like two hundred even now, dreads still on point with grey running through. "Stop acting jealous," She said.

"What the fuck is up man?" Dallas hugged him. It had been way too long. He used to run tough will Mello, Black and Bust. Last he heard Bust crazy ass moved over to China, got married and had some foreign kids. Carmen was even living in the islands with a bad bitch.

"I can't call it, just blessed to be here." Medallion thought about all the hell he caused in the streets. He didn't think he would make it but here he was alive and well.

"Hell ain't we all," Dallas nudged Venom thinking of the hell raiser she used to be.

"Let's go inside so I can give you the details. Then you can get back to the hotel to get settled in with the crew for dinner tonight. Vicious and Black will be joining them as well." Venom was taking the whole crew out to dinner.

"That sound great." Dallas was already enjoying this trip; he had his peoples with him. The trio entered the house it was much better on the inside. A Mid-Century modern home, it's in one of the best areas of Beverly Hills. Sleek, classy design with top quality finishes throughout the place.

High beamed ceilings, accented by skylights. Natural hardwood floors and custom Italian kitchen and bathroom. It only had three bedrooms. One converted to the office. Two thousand two hundred sixty-three square feet. Priced at two million two hundred fifty thousand dollars.

It wasn't nothing Dallas could see himself buying. He needed more bang for his buck. St. Louis greedy ass was better than this. Medallion had to take a business call, so he bid Dallas a goodbye until this even at dinner.

Venom entered the business office after him closing the door. "I never liked this house, but it was the best I could fine. I hate everything about this place," She told him causing him to laugh. He knew she moved there for Vicious.

"When are you coming home then?" Dallas asked.

"Soon as we handle this business," She smiled. She couldn't wait to get the hell out of there.

Chapter 27

Dallas checked into his room wearing the terry cloth bathrobe and slippers. Puffing on a Cuban he picked up the three multi-line telephone calling his crew. His suite was the best, a step back in time luxurious Historic Suite. Green silk, red velvet and hints of gold are found throughout the suite. It overlooks the lush gardens.

The suite also features a separate sitting room 46" Bang & Olufsen BeoVision flat screen television, gourmet mini bar, complimentary fruit/water. A beautiful master bedroom with two full bathrooms. His room was the shit for real. Venom had him setup like a boss. She knew his style. She made sure he would feel like he was at home.

The crew's phone rang and everyone clicked in one by one.

"Hello," Jay said.

"Who is dis?" Jasmine asked causing Dallas to laugh.

"What's up?" Dizzy said.

"Talk to me?" Mack said.

"Speak," Zane was the last to connect with the team. It amazed Dallas see so many personalities amongst his team.

"I am glad to have all of you on this line…" He was cut off.

"We all on this bitch together?" Mack asked.

"Yes we are," Dallas said.

"This hotel the shit," Mack liked this top of the line shit. He was going to have to bring Tasha here after she has the baby.

"Tonight we're having dinner with the head team. I will not talk about the details of the case over the phone. I will tell you guys about it after dinner and you get comfortable. Then return to my suite for the details," Dallas told them.

"So what time is dinner?" Jay asked.

"Seven, formal attire. I suggest you all should go shopping," He said.

"Oh shit," They all chimed hanging up on him to go find what they needed. Dallas laughed because he knew his crew wanted to impress the top dogs.

Jasmine and Jay jumped in the cab trying to find something the never thought they would never need. "Where the fuck do you get a formal dress?" Jasmine asked.

"I don't know hell I am trying to think where the hell I will get a plus size one?" Jay was stressing for real.

"Bitch we're going to find something," Jasmine assured her.

"Aye driver we need some fancy ass clothing for dinner," She handed him a hundred-dollar bill.

"I am on it my friend," He said knowing the perfect place.

The guys on the other had called the front desk asking for formal attire. The desk assistant told them to come down to lobby so they could be fitted and pick the color suit they need. They were glad they didn't have to go far to find what they need. They were chilling in Dallas's room in robes waiting for their clothing. All except Zane, he saw a woman, and he had her give him a message.

Dallas looked at his men it amazed him how much they have grown. He remembered when they all were struggling punks. Look at them now bossing up in Beverly Hills, Ca. Mack and Zane was laughing, talking shit, and smoking Cubans. Mack felt Dallas staring at him, "Man what the hell's wrong with you?" He didn't like no nigga staring at him like that.

"Nigga chill your ass out. I'm just happy we all made it," Dallas laughed.

Zane gave him some dap. "I agree nigga cause some days I wondered if we were going to make it back," He said.

"Nigga what the hell you mean you was stressed? I am the muthafucka that keeps getting shot and shit!" Mack was pissed off about that shit. "I feel like you muthafuckas stopped covering me once the girls joined," His feeling was hurt.

"Man that shit ain't fair," Zane didn't like the shit he said.

"What ain't fair is me ending up in the damn hospital all the time," Mack pouted.

"Nigga fuck you if that's how you feel then that's what it is," Zane knew this nigga had lost his fucking mind talking that shit.

"That's what it is then nigga," Mack said.

Zane was about to say something when Dallas cut him off. "Nigga we never stop covering you. We had to leave you for dead that's the name of the game we in. Shit was this way before the girls came along. When we thought you was dead in Vegas we killed that man's parents behind that shit. Don't play off like that family, it's not cool," Dallas was dead ass serious.

"I feel that shit," Mack got up hugging the men before getting back to talking shit.

Jasmine and Jay were rushing back to their room with their dresses. It was already 4:30, and the limo would he here at 6:00. She spotted Dizzy talking to the Spa girl. She was giggling like she never talked to a nigga before. She wished she could have brought Korey. She nudged Jay. "Look at his bitch ass," She said.

"Are you back with your husband?" Jay asked.

"Bitch I am," She didn't know what that had to do with anything.

"Well bring your ass on, let that man be. He is not your concern. We need to get dressed now," Jay didn't have time to deal with this bullshit, she had to get fly.

"Bitch you make me sick," Jasmine followed her.

"Well bring your sick ass on," Jay said pressing the button on the elevator. Jasmine hustled behind her knowing they were pressed for time.

"Baby I really appreciated how you took care of me back there," Dizzy said thinking about how she released the freak after he dropped a little game on her.

"I don't do this often. I don't want you to think I am that kind of girl," She wasn't lying. She always planned to bag a man that could afford to stay in a place like this. Yet the ones she came across often did way too much. Dizzy was different, she could tell he was balling but had a great heart.

"Girl I don't give a fuck if you did it every day of the week you weren't my woman. Niggas got you women's head fucked up with your hoe if you do this. I am not that kind of nigga. I like to think the G in me made you do it," He schooled her. He wasn't on no little boy ass shit.

"Dizzy you're something else," She smiled wanting to ask to see him again.

"I want to see you again, but it won't be on this trip. Not because I am trying to play you but because I will be leaving in the next twenty-four hours. I am only here on business," He handed her a card with his number on it.

"I hope to see you soon," She held on to the card like it was a key to the city.

"You will baby," He kissed her goodbye.

Chapter 28

Shannon was feeling better; she had hung out with Tasha since the crew had been gone. They talked about her wedding. She was planning to have it in a few months yet now that seemed so far away. She called her mother Marilyn, "Good morning baldhead."

"What do you want Shannon?" This child has always gotten on her nerves the most out of all her children. Yet she loved her and was blessed the day she made it out of the hospital yet again.

"Girl don't do me," Shannon loved to annoy and fight with her mom. It was her own special way of saying I love you.

"I am about to hang up," Marilyn said.

"No mama for real," Shannon knew she better stop playing.

"What is it?" Marilyn asked.

"I am supposed to get married in three months, but I don't want to wait," Shannon said.

"Well then don't wait Shannon," Marilyn stood behind whatever her children wanted if it's right.

"You don't think that's too fast to make it beautiful like I want it?" Shannon asked.

"I have done thirty day weddings for people with a small budget. If you have the money you can do whatever you want no matter how soon you want to do it," Marilyn was a go getter. That was her motto in life; if you want it go get.

"I have the money. I will call Zane to see what he thinks," She informed her.

"Where is Zane?" Marilyn was being nosey.

"Away on business," She said knowing her mother was fishing.

"Is that the same business trip Jasmine on?" Marilyn asked knowing she would not get the details.

"I don't know what you're talking about. I will call you when I am ready to start planning," Shannon shut her down. She knew Korey had told her Jasmine left again.

"Bye Shannon," Marilyn laughed.

"Bye," Shannon hung up.

Zane's head was hurting. He'd drank way too much wine and smoked too many Cubans with the guys at dinner last night. He never imagined doing all the things he has been blessed to do. God shed his light on him for sure. He got out of bed naked to take an aspirin. Even though his head was hurting he smiled thinking about last night.

The limo arrived about 6:45 p.m. The men were waiting in the lobby all dressed to kill. Dallas had on a three button, black herringbone 5/16 top stich lapels, center vent patched pocket, magenta twill silk lined jacket with matching shirt. With a single reserved pleated trouser matching the jacket. To finish the look, he chose smoked grey cordovan low vamp loafers.

Mack was rocking Peal & Co extended strap loafers with a grey sharkskin suit. Narrow lapels, a shorter jacket length with two-buttons and side vents with signature striped lining.

Dizzy was fresh to death in an elegant fit tuxedo impeccably tailored for a luxurious drape slim fit. Featuring satin-covered lapels and one button and Edward Green Piccadilly leather loafers.

Zane shut shit down in the velvet crown slippers, Micro check suit, and jacket made from pure wool woven in Italy. Modern fit, lapels, and signature striped lining. The guys were on point all thank to the front desk's work and Brooks Brothers clothing line.

The guys were loading up in the limo when Jasmine arrived stopping traffic in a Leather trim stretch lace gown. This head-

turning gown was stunning black lace with double shoulder straps. Plunging V-neck, cut-out front detail, glittery waist insets. Deep front slit, crisscross back straps with back zip closure hugging her just right. She paired an Athena Trillion statement necklace and earrings set, and Casadei peplum back leather pumps.

Jay joined them in her Tadashi Shoji boat neck paneled gown. Sheer lace, and pin tucked panels creating texturally rich, slimming gown sleeveless, concealed back zip. She picked an Allen Schwartz necklace and earring with Alexander Wang leather pumps. Thanks to Saks Fifth Avenue the women stole the show. All Dallas could do was smile at his team's growth as the headed over to "The Ivy" restaurant.

The phone ringing in the bedroom broke his train of thought. He knew it wasn't time to case the bank. That's wasn't due until noon time, high traffic hours. They were planning to make their move an hour before closing, low traffic hours. "Hello?"

"Why the hell you didn't answer your phone?" Shannon asked.

"Did you call here to argue about a phone?" He need to know cause if she did, she was about the be arguing with the dial tone.

"No I didn't smart ass," Shannon knew he wasn't in the mood to fight.

"I love you too. Now state your business," He said.

"I don't want to wait months to get married. I want to do it now; I might as well get it out the way while the baby in the hospital. Once she home I won't have time to think about a wedding," She didn't tell him about the funny feeling that something might cause them to never get married.

"Shannon how soon you talking?" He knew he wasn't gone win, and she had a point.

"In three weeks. Mom said she has done weddings in thirty days for people with a low budget. So we should be a shoe in for three weeks," Shannon was excited. He could hear it in her voice.

"It's like this if we do it you will have to wait on something." He said.

"Wait on what?" She asked.

"Getting a wedding ring or house. You have a huge ass engagement ring but it's a few years old. You know how you women are about rings. Yet we need more space for the baby. I am not going broke with a wedding, ring, and home. I know we paid but until this new shit start paying out we got to spend wisely," Zane told her.

"I can wait on the ring but no more than a year," She said.

"I didn't say I need that long. I am a boss but cool," He needed her to check his resume.

"Whatever, how is it out there?" She was a little worried about him.

"It's going well. We move tonight then we out of here," He assured her.

"That's what up. I guess I will go plan for my wedding," She said.

"Shannon stop worrying. Go call Tasha and start planning and don't spend too much of my money in the next twenty-four hours," He knew he needed to get home to watch their spending.

"I love you baby," She said.

"I love you too boo," He smiled.

"Bye I got money to spend," She teased.

"Bye crazy," He hung up looking at the clock it was only 8:15 a.m. He set his alarm for 10:00 a.m., then headed back to sleep.

Roc was laid up with Mariah when Dallas called him to tell him where his team should be if needed. Roc assured him his men was on top of things as he watched Mariah naked ass jiggle as she went to the bathroom. He ended the call with Dallas lying in bed stroking his dick, "Mariah come back to bed with big daddy." The girl had good pussy on her. His baby mama had been calling all day, but he wasn't trying to fuck with her. She was back up pussy when the bitch he wanted to fuck was acting, yet he always takes care of the kids.

"No baby I am ready to head home," She was getting the plan in motion with Q.

"Baby why don't you just leave here with me? Leave that madness behind," He was feeling her more than she knew. They were great together. He had never fell for a woman this fast. He'd been with her since the night they went for dinner.

"I can't do that. I am ready to go," She liked him but not enough to change her plans. Jay and all her friends would pay for what she'd done.

"Damn we only been together two days," He was fussing.

"Sounds like you're sprung," She had to laugh at him. It was cute she never had a man want her around like this.

"Girl please," He jumped out the bed thinking *"She ain't about play me like no sucker."* He was in his feelings and Mariah could tell.

"I am sorry Roc. I just need to holler at my uncle then we can come back to the hotel if you want," She kissed him rubbing his semi hard dick through his pants.

"I am with that if that's what you want to do," He was trying to play it cool.

"Yes baby that what I want to do," She assured him.

"Cool I will go check on my kids. Call me when you're ready," He said putting on his shoes.

"Kids better be the only thing you checking on too," She said pulling her shirt over her head. She was thinking about what he said about her leaving with him. It had a nice ring to it. She didn't really want to spend the rest of her life looking over her shoulder. She was learning many people do things in life to survive. It's business not personal.

"Oh so you jealous? You don't trust a nigga?" He picked her up slamming her on the bed kissing her.

She looked into his eyes. "I don't trust no nigga," She said.

"Let me change that for you," He could see the hurt in her eyes. He knew she had been let down so many times. Roc wanted to show her there was more to life. He tried to share this with his kid's mother, but she can't see passed the hood. He could tell that Mariah was sick of this hood shit, she just had no way out.

She pushed him off of her. "I don't like people making promises they can't keep," The things he said sounded good to her. She just wasn't strong enough to get her hopes up high to be let down again.

"The only thing stopping me from keeping my promise is you," He wanted her to know he was for real about everything he speaks.

"I hear you," She said as she opened the hotel door to exit. She was really considering what he was saying. It was hard to accept such an offer knowing she would depend on him.

Q was wondering where the hell Mariah had been for the last two days. He was getting worried when she walked in the house with a magical glow. He knew that glow well. She had been fucked good and was on the verge of falling in love. "Where the hell you been?" he asked.

"Out!" She yelled, wondering who the hell he thought he was to question her about her whereabouts.

"Out with who?" Q asked.

"Roc, why you all in my business?" She wasn't feeling him questioning her.

"I told him to take you out, not fuck your brain out. Now you're coming up in here talking to me like you crazy," Q didn't know what the hell was wrong with her. Nor did he plan for the two to hit it off so well.

"Cash I am grown," She called his name out not thinking.

"I told you don't call me that. You never know who is listening or watching." He said.

"Right I don't. I am not feeling this lying low shit anymore. I want my revenge on Jay, yet I don't even feel it's worth wasting the time on," She had to get that off her chest. She wasn't just saying this because of Roc. Mariah was tired of all this bullshit going on around her. Yes, she has lost so much, yet hunting Jay won't bring what she lost back. She needed to change her life for the better. The first thing she was planning to do was shake Q/Cash's ass.

"Bitch you don't let that nigga get in your head that fast," He was often disrespectful to her all her life.

"Oh yeah, that's the Cash I been waiting to show up." Mariah would often leave home when he acted this way. It was part of the reason she often took disrespect from her child's father. Hell if she thought about it, the only time he didn't flip out on her was when he was with Jay for that short while.

"I didn't mean to say that. I just saying how you going to back out on me now?" He didn't need her help, he just wanted to control her. Truth was he didn't want to hurt Jay, but he felt if he couldn't have her no one will.

"I am not backing out I am just saying it's not worth it," She yelled at him while she texts Roc.

"Come get me now," She sent the message. She had her phone volume off so when he texts back Cash wouldn't know.

The message icon popped up on the top of the phone. *"I am on my way baby."* He hadn't even made it to his kids. When he called to say he was coming by his baby mama said she had company. He wasn't in the mood for her shit so he fell back, stopping at the corner store. He didn't know what was going on with Mariah but he was coming for her.

"Thanks." She texts back.

Q wondered why the hell she keeps looking at the phone. He walked over snatching it out her had. "What hell is on this phone that's so important?"

Mariah punched his ass in the face. "Give me my dam phone," Taking it back from him.

"So you gone hit me? Get the fuck out my house. Do what you want to do. When that nigga plays you don't come crawling back," He said wanting beat her ass, but he wasn't gone do that.

"I am outside." Mariah read the text looking at her uncle, "I will gladly leave this bitch." She didn't know how she would make it out there. Yet she knew for the time being that Roc would be the nigga he claims to be. He was going to make smart moves to secure her when he was ready to leave or play games.

Mariah slammed the door on her way out. The painting on the wall fell shattering the glass. Q didn't know how his life had come to this. Yet the person responsible for it all was enjoying life in sunny California. Mariah didn't have to help him. Jay will pay no matter what.

Chapter 30

"We're looking for 9593 Wilshire Boulevard at Dayton Way, Beverly Hills, CA 90212," Zane told Dallas as he whipped the rental.

"Right there nigga." The bank sat on the corner at a stop. That was great because you can get in and out faster.

"Alright," Dallas parked the car at the meter. He hopped out while Zane dropped change in the meter. They weren't planning to be in the bank long. Just needed to case the place to see what kind of holdup they were dealing with first hand. If anyone ever tried to rob a bank without casing the place, they were setting their team up for failure.

The moment they entered the bank they could tell this shit was gone be easier than taking candy from a baby. This place wasn't huge. Four tellers and two attendants starting new accounts. It was midday, a little past noon. The bank was packed so all the teller windows were opened. Dallas could tell by their set up, at closing two tellers shut down.

He looked for the vault to see what could use to get back there smoothly. Zane walked over to one of the accountings, "I am thinking of opening an account if I move here." He hit her with that St. Louis accent.

She was a young black woman and very impressionable. One thing she loved about living in Beverly Hills succeeded men. She didn't care what race; all money was green. She had slept with a few good men here or there but none fine as Zane. "I am Tamika Lowes and I would be glad to help you out." She looked over at Dallas "Will he be opening account as well?" Zane looked at Dallas.

"Nah he is with me," He said. By the look on her face he could tell she thought he meant as a couple.

"We have great stock holders in the gay community," She said thinking, *"Damn all the fine ones rich and gay."*

"That's great. I will have to speak to my wife about that when I get back home. She's been looking for ways to support the gay community," He assured her he wasn't gay.

"I am so sorry I never meant to offend you sir," Tamika was glad his fine ass wasn't gay, but she gave no fucks about him being married. If she would be a side chick the nigga better have six figures if not more to spend on her.

"That's fine. I am not offended at all love. Now can you show me what your bank has to offer?" Zane said.

"Yes right this way," She walked in front of him over to her desk. She had an ass like a stripper; she killed that pencil skirts she was wearing.

Zane walked behind her shaking his head as that ass jiggled like Jell-O. *"Lord I love my wife,"* He whispered to himself as he followed her.

Dallas was looking around to check to see how many guards was on duty, and if they were armed. He spotted two armed guards with revolvers. He knew they wasn't going to be able to handle his crew. He didn't understand why banks didn't give all the guards and teller heat. Hell if he owned a bank everyone would be concealed to carry, trained and licensed to shoot.

In less than fifteen minutes Zane was waving him over to leave. Dallas was reading brochures just to look innocent. He walked over to Zane looking at the paperwork he was holding his hand. He knew that everything went as planned with Zane opening the new account under false information Venom had made up for them.

The two men excited the car just in time to see the meter maid about to give them a ticket. "Hey love," Dallas said. She looked at the two good looking men.

"This your car?" She smiled her plumped cheeks at them.

"Yeah that's me," Dallas said to the beautiful plus size lady.

"I am going to have to give you a ticket," She was polite, just doing her job.

"How much is the ticket?" Dallas asked.

"I am going to say it's going to be five hundred dollars," She said.

"Damn everything high in Cali for real," He said handing her five hundred dollars.

"What is this?" She asked.

"Take that and keep the ticket beautiful." He meant that not trying to uplift her cause she was on the heavier side. This woman was really breathe taking.

"I am not supposed to do this, but I guess this one time won't hurt. Plus, it's my birthday," She said.

"Well on that note here is another five hundred. Buy yourself something as sweet as you," Dallas told her.

"Thank you sir, thank you so much." She wasn't use to nice looking men showing her respect, yet from now on she was demanding nothing less.

"You are truly welcome," Dallas opened his are door. She walked away whistling.

Zane hoped in the car. "Man that was G of you. Her little cute fat ass too happy," Zane said cause Dallas to laugh.

"Got to keep a smile on all the women's face. God made me just for that," Dallas thought he was god's gift to woman. He handles them with care, instead of force. His grandmother raised him until she died when he was sixteen. She would always say "You catch more flies with honey verse shit." His grandmother was a handful for sure. He missed her on days like this.

"Nigga please. Where are we heading now?" Zane asked.

"To the hotel. What we needed to move this evening has already been delivered," Dallas assured him.

"What time we pulling out of this city?" He knew they didn't layover in any city after a hit.

"Midnight," Dallas told him.

"Indeed," Zane figured that much.

Dallas pulled in traffic ready to handle this business then head home. The hotel was dope, but he missed his own bed.

Jay and Jasmine met Mack in his room. He called telling them a package had been delivered to this room for them. The girls didn't know what the hell they needed for this hit but they were about to find out. Jasmine knocked on the door. Mack yelled, "Man bring y'all ass in."

"I am going to knock your ass out one day," Jasmine said as she walked into the room.

"Why wait?" He grabbed her slamming on the bed.

"Nigga you got me messed up," She jumped off the bed swinging on him. Jay was stealing on that fool too.

"Damn y'all gone jump me in my own room?" He said covering his head from the blows.

They busted out laughing, "Nigga damn right." They both hugged him.

"What the fuck they send us?" Jay asked.

"All black attire, shirt, pants, shoes, and face masks. Also custom made, all black MCM duffle bags. Oh yeah and these pretty bitches," He pulled out three Winchester model twelve hundred, stainless steel, pump action, twelve gauge shotguns. Factory nineteen-inch barrel, folding rear sight, bead front sight, and sling swivels handles.

"These muthafuckas could knock an elephant on its ass with no problem," Jay snatched it out his hand. "Damn this bitch sexy," She said stroking it.

"Girl be careful that ain't no dick. This shit will blow your brains out," He laughed.

"Nigga fuck you," Jay had to laugh with him.

"Okay so how we moving?" Jasmine asked. She needed details.

"Dallas and Zane going in as the health inspectors. That way they will have access to the vault and deposit boxes. Once they have been there for about twenty minute we move in robbing the bank. Whatever money we get out that bitch Venom said the three of us can split. All she wants is what's in the safe deposit box. I say we share it with the whole team, getting a cut on top of what she pays us," Mack stated.

"The bank robbery is diversion from what's really being taken?" Jay asked.

"Yes," Mack said.

"What time we move?" Jasmine asked.

"Dallas and Zane go in at 6:00 p.m. because the bank closes at 7:00 p.m. We move in at 6:30 p.m. allowing them enough time to get in the back."

"I am with that. So do we pull out to tonight?" Jay asked.

"Layover will get you fucked over. You know we out of here at midnight," Mack school her.

"I guess we better go pack," Jasmine said.

"Yeah our bags will be picked up at 5:00 p.m. and taken to the jet."

The girls headed out the room to pack. When they made it to their rooms Jay looked at Jasmine. "You ready to die?" She asked because Shannon wasn't here to ask.

"Not yet ask me later," Jasmine said as she entered her room. She was so glad this was her last job

Zane was looking dapper in his business suit. It was nothing to write home about like the brooks brothers suit he wore the other night, yet he was still looking good for a health inspector. Tamika was just a pawn in his plan. She will remember him from earlier that day. He was hoping the crew didn't have to lay a muthafucka down. He didn't understand how people risked their life for money that's insured and not theirs.

Hell if he worked in a bank they could bet their ass he wouldn't be the hero that saves the day. Fuck that shit. Nothings that deep to fuck around a get your head blow off for some bullshit.

The phone in his bedroom rang, and he knew it was time to move. He looked at the clock it said 5:30 p.m. Zane picked up the phone "Hello?"

"Sir your car has arrived," The front desk clerks stated.

"I am heading down now," He said hanging the phone walking past the mirror, clipping his name badge on to his jacket. *"It's show time,"* He said to himself heading out the door.

Dallas was already in the car by the time Zane made it down. The driver opened the door allowing his to get in. Once Zane was inside he closed the door then jumped in to the driver's seat. He pulled of heading to the location already locked into his GPS. "Man I thought you had changed your mind on me," Dallas teased him.

"Nigga never that. I see you fresh and clean too," Dallas also had a name badge on for the California Health Department.

"It ain't Brooks Brothers but it's cool," He popped his collar.

"I said the same shit when I was up in the room," Zane laughed.

"Well it time to get this money," Dallas said.

"Yes indeed it is." The driver was pulled up in front of the bank. He was about to get out to open the door.

"No stay put, we got it," He told the driver. He knew somewhat of what was going down. He worked for Venom, yet he knew no major details.

"Yes sir," He said.

The duo hopped out the car heading into the bank. Dallas received a text from Mack upon entering the bank. *"We two blocks down form the bank."* He hit Dallas up after Jay informed him they arrived. She had been watching the bank through the scoop on her shotgun. Jay was perched on top of the building directly across the street from the bank.

Dallas read the text then responded "I will let you know when we in the back," He sent the message shoving the throw away phone back in his pocket. There were ten people in the bank. They weren't expecting it to be this busy, but the show must go on. It was now or never. Zane walked over to Tamika's desk. "Remember me?" He asked.

"Yeah I do," She smiled but something was different. His clothing was cheaper.

"I am head of the board inspector/quality control for the Health Department of California. This is my partner," He said handing her the paperwork with his badge.

"That's great." She knew she should have been on her best behavior and not flirting all the time. She hoped she would not lose her damn job. Her sponsor got married yesterday telling her he no longer wanted to see her. She had to pay for her condo and BMW with her own money now until she replaced him.

"I will be needing to see your safe deposit box area. That's all I need to approve in order for this bank to remain open for business," He said.

She was glad as hell to hear him say that. "Say no more I will lead the way," Tamika was glad she took the evening shift as night manager. If Bob, the day manger was here he would be all in the damn way. She wanted their ass in and out. "Here we are, call me if you need me. I can't leave the bank unattended," She was the only manager here and two tellers.

"It won't take long," Zane assured her.

She walked out to the front thinking, "Good so I can get the hell out of here." She wasn't in the mood for this shit today.

The moment Dallas could tell the coast was clear. He grabbed the phone out of his pocket text Mack. *"It's time to move. We're in the back."*

Mack responded *"10-4"*, then he looked at Jasmine. "It's time to move."

"Let go," She hopped out the car with the shotgun in one hand, duffle bag in the other. Yes, it was broad day light, and these masked fools were walking down the streets of Beverly Hills with heavy equipment. They knew the cops would arrive soon from the looks people gave them as they crossed the street heading toward the bank.

"Box 764," Dallas said to Zane as he looked out to make sure Tamika wasn't coming.

"Got it." Zane had a great eye for shit like this.

"Code 1738," Dallas said hoping that Mack moved in soon so he could help Zane.

Zane hit the code fast as he could watch the door pop open. "Oh my lord," Zane needed Jesus to help him right now. Dallas was still looking out when he heard, *"Everybody one the ground."* It was still six customers in the bank.

The gate to deposit box closed and Dallas knew the robbery has taken place. The workers were taught to cut off access to the big money. Then signal the alarm from behind the desk. "Yes, they're here. What the hell are you calling on the lord for?" he walked over to see what Zane was stuck looking at. Dallas couldn't believe his eyes. Ten gold bars, all worth a million each. "Holy shit," Zane finally said.

"I know right. I can't believe these are real gold bars," Dallas had never seen no shit like this in his life.

Zane popped the briefcase he had with him. "Let's load these up so we can lock this shit back up before they let us out of here."

"Load them up." Dallas grabbed the cold, golden bars placing them in the briefcase.

Mack had the shotgun on the tellers. Jasmine threw a duffle bag at each. "Fill up the fucking bag," They came at the perfect time the cash cow was out.

Tamika was in the bathroom when the robbery took place. She didn't know what was going on, but she was ready to go. She was about to check for the men in the back when she turned around facing a shotgun. She didn't need this shit today in her bank. The teller was filling the bags up with a lot of money. She would not take the blame for this shit.

Tamika reach over to hit the silent alarm. Her eyes grew big as saucers as her chest exploded from the shot Jasmine put in her chest. Mack had to close his eye for a minute after seeing that. He didn't really want to hurt anyone today. "Fill up the fucking bag,"

Jasmines yelled hopping off the desk throwing the first filled bag to Mack.

"Man hurry up." He yelled at the teller. She was shaken up after seeing her boss killed. She filled bag to the rim, zipping it then tossed it to them. As they were moving out of the bank you could hear the sirens closing in. Jay spotted the first police rushing to the scene. She pulled the trigger blowing out his tired causing his car to flip. More cops were coming as she let off more shots. She watched Jasmine and Mack haul ass to the getaway car.

The last shot Jay released blew a cop's head clean off. As she watched Mack speed off hitting the highway heading to the hide out spot. Jay packed her gun up inside her duffle bag heading to the getaway spot as will. She had to say this was good mission.

Chapter 32

The cops didn't know what the hell hit their city. Things like this rarely happened here. When it did, it was an amateur move. This here that had taken place today was one hundred percent professional. Dallas and Zane were discovered in the back. After showing the proper documents and explaining they were locked in the back from the moment the robbery took place they could go. They were even escorted out the building by a cop for their safety.

The driver was still parked in the same spot. He never moved even the shooting took place because he was safe. All of Venom's cars are fully bullet proof. Dallas and Zane hopped in the car heading over to the getaway spot. Zane couldn't believe they pulled this shit off. He had to admit he was going to miss these missions. He was about be a family man. He couldn't keep risking his life doing shit like this. Zane knew that he would never be out the game. Now he was just going to become low key.

Dizzy had been at the getaway spot since 5:00 p.m. He loaded the luggage on to the jet then waited out front for the crew. He had the easiest job this run, and he could live with that. He was tired of living in a war zone. Mack and Jasmine were the first to get there. Jay arrived about twenty minutes later. They'd got five hundred thousand off the bank.

"I shouldn't have killed her," Jasmine demons was already haunting her.

"Sis you had to," Mack didn't want to see the young girl die either. This was business, never personal.

"Man let that shit go. It is what it is," Jay didn't harp over the lives she took. She asked for forgiveness after each one. She was going to let god be the judge of her wrong doing when the time come.

"Bravo." the sound of Venom voice causes the whole room to look up. As she walked in with Dallas and Zane.

"Thank you," The crew chimed. Jasmine was the last to shed her attire as Dizzy set it all on fire in a metal trash can.

"No really you guys and girls are a force to be reckoned with. Hell I needed y'all on my team when I was heavy in the game," Venom was proud of this crew's skills.

"We owe this all to Dallas," Jay said.

"Like hell you do girl you been putting work since day one," Venom told Jay.

"Thank you," Jay said.

She looked at Jasmine. "Don't sweat the small shit. You shot her, but you didn't kill her cause you're not the giver of life. It was her time to go you just helped her along the way," Venom said to her.

"I needed to hear that," Jasmine said.

"We can do lunch when I moved back home," She said. Jasmine and Jay agreed. "Good, you all are free to go," She said.

It was 9:00 p.m. Cali time, 11:00 p.m. St. Louis time. They would make it home after midnight as planned. Dallas was the only person still in the getaway house with Venom.

"This is it huh?" He had to ask because he couldn't believe that it was over.

"Yeah this is it, we've come a long way my nigga," Venom was a little emotional.

"That we did. I hope we will still see each other even though it's not about business anymore," Dallas said wanting his old friend back.

"We family for life," Venom hugged him.

"I love you girl," He let a tear fall without her knowing.

"I love you more baby," She released him and he walked away.

"See you when I get home," She yelled.

"Indeed," He was walking away from his old life into a new. He didn't know where it would lead him. Dallas was glad to leave the past behind, ready to embark on a bright future.

Epilogue

Three Months Later

Zane was standing in the dressing room of the Four Seas Banquet Facility. Today was the big day; he was about to marry his queen. He looked handsome in his Golden Fleece Tails Tuxedo, elegant formal wear all white traditional tailed coat, cream vest and bowtie with pleat-front trousers. Allen Edmonds pebble leather wingtips white shoes and gold and white hand painted enamel cuff links and Brooks Brothers 1818 signature cologne completed his attire. He was as ready as he would ever be.

Venom sent the five million she promised the team. Along with the five hundred thousand from the bank. Dallas split it evenly amongst the crew. Shannon didn't have to wait for her ring. She didn't know that yet, he wants to surprise her on this special day of hers. He was ready for the honeymoon in the Bahamas. The knock at the door startled him a little, "Come in." It was Dallas.

"Looking good man, but it's time to get this show on a road." He knew he had been held up in the room to long and someone would come get him sooner or later.

"I am ready," He said.

"Are you really?" Dallas had to ask. No one from the crew had ever did anything like this.

"No, but who else will I find better to spend my life with?" He said.

"No one," Dallas assured him.

"Thank man for everything," Zane meant that. Without this man he wouldn't be the man he was today.

"I am honored, now let's go," He said he didn't want the man catching cold feet.

"Let's go." They headed into the hall.

Jay was running late and Jasmine had been calling her like crazy. She assured them she was on the way. She didn't know that Q had been listening to all her calls for the last couple of months. He had plans for this wedding they all would never forget. He was left to handle this alone since Mariah ran off with Roc. He heard the nigga was up in New York somewhere. He didn't really care about what they had going, all he wanted to do was end Jay's life and today was the day.

The hall was located just west of Soulard and south of the Lafayette Park. Jay arrived right on time. The wedding was due to start in twenty minutes. Even though the place could hold four hundred, Shannon only had her three girls Jasmine, Jay, and Tasha. Her mother, and all the duffle bag men. She even allowed Dizzy to bring the girl he met at the spa in Cali. They'd been traveling back and forward since the trip.

Jay walked in the place and it was beautiful. Fourteen foot ceilings with black accented white drapes stretching from the exquisite terrazzo floor to the ceiling accentuated with soft, beautiful lights. The entire facility sprinkled with dim lights to create the perfect ambience. The twelve-piece band was a nice touch. She headed to a table with white linen table cloths, cushioned banquet chairs and white linen chair covers with cream bows on the back of each chair.

The tables were preset with china and silverware. With mirrored rounds, vases of beautiful flowers, and tea light candles. The place was amazing. Zane was standing under the arch waiting for Shannon to arrive. The band played music. Shannon was walking down the red carpet she asked to be placed down when she about to enter. The moment Shannon was halfway an explosion cause the whole front end of the hall to collapse.

Jay was screaming, "Oh god noooo."

Q could hear the people screaming on the inside as he put down the gas can he used to pour gas around the outside. He threw a matching watching the place go up in flame. He smiled hopping in his car hoping they all burned in hell.

The End

I want to thank everyone for supporting me through this series. It has been the most amazing stories I ever written. Don't focus on this being the end. Think of it as a new beginning for the characters you have grown to love in this book.

CPSIA information can be obtained
at www.ICGtesting.com
Printed in the USA
LVHW08s1747210918
590922LV00010B/611/P

9 781534 603998